THE HIDDEN CITY

Book 2 of The Great Devastation Trilogy

THE HIDDEN CITY

Book 2 of The Great Devastation Trilogy

DANA PRIDE

Everlasting Publishing
Yakima, Washington
USA

The Hidden City

by
Dana Pride

Book 2 of The Great Devastation Trilogy

Library of Congress Control Number
2013940200

ISBN: 0-9852739-6-8

ISBN-13: 978-0-9852739-6-5

First Edition
Everlasting Publishing
P.O. Box 1061
Yakima, WA 98907

I could not leave Layla and her father in the desert forever; thus "The Hidden City," Book 2 of The Great Devastation Trilogy, was created.

For my family,
Thank you for your encouragement
all along the way.

Dana

THE HIDDEN CITY

CHAPTER 1

When I opened my eyes that morning, I thought for a moment that I was still dreaming. The lighting in the room was unnaturally natural, my bed was strangely comfortable, and the air I was breathing was real; not re-circulated, refined, compressed, conditioned air, but air from the Outside, natural air. I couldn't hear the subliminal message music that played throughout the Complex twenty-four hours per day, but I could hear the sound of something else, something natural, the wind, maybe? Also, I couldn't feel the comforting hug of my sleeper, but I felt like I was wearing clothing — clothes that were not my own.

Suddenly, it all came back to me in a wonderful rush: I was Outside, I was somewhere across the world, and I was in a sort of a tent with my dad! This was all real, not a dream! Yesterday, the day I found my dad, seemed to be a dream; yet it had all happened. My dear friend, Kenrick, had brought me all the way across the world, secretly, back to where The Great Devastation had happened nine years ago, back to the place I had lived and where I had last seen my dad, the place where I was sure he had been killed in that horrible war. Then a force, must have been the Spirit of God, guided me alone to the place where my dad had been living all this time, and back into his arms, back into his life.

My life immediately changed yesterday, as I knew I could not go back to the Complex, and I needed to live here, with the only family member I had, not in a controlled, organized, indoor facsimile of a life where I played games for a living, games which had no consequence except to keep me busy. I could not go back to a place where someone was choosing a mate for me, where my name had been thrown "in the mix," where I had no say about the main person who would be sharing my life. No, my life was now here, with my dad. After all, I was still a child, only seventeen years old, and I needed my dad. I needed to be a child again, not a young child, but his daughter. I needed to have my father with me. We could never regain the years we had lost, but we could start now — we had already started — to make up for lost time, lost hugs, lost joy, lost love.

As the world came into focus, my new world, the real world, I saw my dad sitting on a stool across the hut. He was gazing at me, giving me a look that only a dad can give to his daughter. He had a slight smile and nothing but love and concern in his eyes.

"Daddy," I said hoarsely. My voice was not quite awake yet.

"My La-la," he said, speaking his nickname for me. "How did you sleep?"

"I thought it was all a dream," I said, clearing my throat, "but it was real. I am really here with you!"

"I was almost afraid to go to sleep," he said, "because I didn't want you to fade away like you did so many times in my dreams. Only in my dreams, I didn't see you as this grown up girl you are! I imagined a bit of aging, but you didn't get much older than you were the last time I saw you. Now I see you, my beautiful daughter, and I can't imagine you any other way. You don't know how happy I am that you are here."

"Daddy — it is the best feeling in the world to be able to say that again! Daddy! Daddy! My dad! Daddy, I am so happy to be here. The missing part of my life is not missing any more! You are here!" I forgot what I was going to say — my eyes filled with tears, my chest was all choking.

Dad's eyes were filling also. I could not remember ever seeing him cry — except yesterday, that is. He grabbed a cloth from a small pile of clothing and handed it to me, and got one for himself as well. I dabbed my eyes as he blew his nose. The real world was coming back to me as I considered these handkerchiefs. These were to be used instead of sanitized, perfumed, sterilized, disposable items like the ones we used back at the Complex in order to get any substance that came out of the body away from us and into a hazard disposal as soon as possible. Nothing 'hazardous' could touch anyone, no one was allowed to touch anyone else. We were isolated, insulated, uncontaminated, unfeeling cogs in a machine that existed in the middle of nowhere, away from any possible enemies or dangers.

Now I was a real person, a person who was allowed to have feelings and even express those feelings without hiding them. I was feeling so emotional after all the years of holding everything inside me, years of trying to not feel, years of substituting artificial feelings for what I was really feeling, and constantly wearing a happy face. I felt like laughing out loud, because of my new freedom, and I did. I burst out laughing, just letting it all come out of my heart, as tears ran down my face. I knew I would not need to explain anything to Dad. I would not have to hide or pretend something was funny or justify my actions. I was allowed to just be myself when I was with my dad!

I recalled the question once being asked, "If I can't be myself, who can I be?" and I thought at the time it was a ridiculous question. How could people be anyone but themselves? Now I knew the answer. When I was not allowed to be myself, all the time I was living and working at the Complex, I was a robot, a drone, a compliant being without feelings or a personality of my own. I was just what they wanted me to be, what they told me to be. Everything was so clear now. My façade of a life, my former life, was now exposed to me, and I felt like I could understand everything, now that I was away from the controllers, the manipulators, the non-feeling leaders of the super-civilized community.

"That's my Layla," Dad said with a smile. "You always had such a sense of humor. You found ordinary things funny, and you would laugh and laugh, and you would make us laugh right along with you. When you thought something was funny, you made us look at it in a new way and we would always laugh about it, too. Some expressions that were so common to us, you thought were so funny, you would laugh every time you heard them.

"I don't know if you remember this, but when you heard someone say 'over the weekend,' you would repeat it, '*over the weekend???*' as if it were the funniest saying in the world, and you would just laugh and laugh. I had the hardest time keeping a straight face when I was at work and someone would tell me what they had done over the weekend. I would just hear your little voice in my head and try my best not to smile, while inside I was just cracking up. I remember one time, during an important meeting, one of my supervisors was discussing what we would have to do over the weekend. I was already somewhat bored of the whole meeting, and my mind easily repeated his phrase in your voice. I had to excuse myself and go into the men's room where I could let loose my laughter. Then I started laughing even harder because it was not such a funny thing, but I was laughing at myself for laughing at something that was not so funny!

"Oh, Layla, I haven't laughed in so many years," Dad said regretfully. "I have missed out on so much of your life, I have missed you so very much… and now you have brought the laughter back to me again. Thank you. I thank God for you. I thank Him so much for bringing you back to me."

"It really was a miracle, wasn't it?"

"It could be nothing less than a miracle, my darling daughter."

"Daddy! I haven't heard that expression in so long, I forgot all about it!" Shame on me for not remembering every detail about my dad, my wonderful dad! He was always the best of dads, and I had allowed myself to forget so many things about him! My busy life in the Complex kept my mind on trivial things, so the important things, the most important things, had slipped away from me, away from my memory. They had made it seem like it was all for the best, the unfeeling ways of life, so we would not be hurting from our memories of Life Before. They didn't realize, for me, at least, Life Before was my only life. Existing in the Complex was not a life at all. I was not a robot! I was a teenage girl with feelings, strong feelings; most of all, a deep love for my family members, the dear ones who had been mercilessly cut out of my life on the Day of Devastation.

"I have thought of little else, in all these years," my dad sighed, "besides my darling daughter and my wonderful wife. My memories of you have sustained me. I often asked God why He had spared my life when all my family had been taken, and the only answer I received was that He still had a reason for me to be alive. He still had work for me to do. I wondered what I could do and how I could do anything when I was not able to speak, so I just waited. I felt that when the time was right, God would show me just what to do, and in the meantime, I was to live in peace with these strangers who took me in and cared for me.

"Speaking of caring for people, you must be hungry! You haven't eaten anything since you arrived, and did you know, that was two days ago?"

"Two days ago?" I asked, puzzled. "No, I just got here yesterday," I reminded him.

He smiled at me, that warm, sweet smile. "You have been asleep since two days ago. I didn't want to awaken you, you were in such a deep sleep."

"I slept for two days?" I asked. I usually slept for only three hours at a time, so this was rather unbelievable.

"Well, not two full days, but you have been asleep since the night before last night. Now it's morning. You slept through an entire day."

"I did? And I didn't even have any dreams!"

"You must have been exhausted."

"You know, I think I just have not genuinely slept in a very long time. At the Complex, I usually just slept in short shifts. And I have not slept in natural, outside air since the day I went into the Complex, nine years ago. Your air smells so good!"

"That would surely make a difference," Dad agreed, "but I must say, it's not my air. The earth is the Lord's and the fullness thereof." He spread his arms to make his point.

"Yes! Oh, and in answer to your question, yes! I am hungry! But first, where is your bathroom?" I suddenly became aware that I was about to burst.

"We have a tent that we move around to different spots, where you have privacy, but it doesn't have a toilet. Come on, I'll take you there. I have always thought of it as our port-a-tent, since it moves around to a fresh spot every couple of days."

Dad led me to the tent and instructed me to dig a little hole with a small shovel that was hanging on a string inside the tent. I felt so adventurous, not worrying about germs and contamination, being outside of a completely clean little box, like we had at the Complex. I was doing something natural in natural surroundings, as opposed to doing something natural in a spotless, man-made tiny room. At the Complex, we were treated like hygienic specimens that could never come in contact with a speck of dirt or dust. I just remembered: I liked dirt! I loved to walk barefoot in the sand! I may be able to do this here, walk in the sand with my dad, in the early morning before the sand would be too hot for the foot to touch.

When I emerged from the tent, Dad was conversing in Arabic with two other men. Although I could only understand a few of the words, I could tell that the men were very surprised that my dad could talk, and that he could speak Arabic. I did understand when Dad told them that I was his daughter, and they looked at me in amazement. I smiled at them, showing them Dad's smile, and they must have had no doubt at that point.

Dad led me to another hut, a larger hut, where a table was set with food. This was real, natural food! I was expecting some of the old food they had scavenged from one of the Four Quadrants storage barns, but this was some type of fresh meat, some fruit that looked like pink apples and red grapes, and a leafy substance. Meat never smelled so good as this, which was roasted and looked to be perfectly tender. Fresh flat loaves of bread were still steaming, in large bowls on the table. I followed Dad's lead and selected a small amount of each food and put it on a clay plate.

We took our meals back to Dad's hut to eat.

"We live in a community here," Dad said. "We each do something to help. One guy is really good at making bread, so he makes bread like this every day. A few others like to cook, and they fix the meals for all of us. Some guys set up the tents when we have to move them, and some hunt and some gather food."

"What do you do?" I asked, taking a bite of the bread, which was delicious and so soft. I knew my dad could do just about anything.

"I help clean up," he said humbly.

I almost couldn't believe my ears. My dad, my hero, the intelligent psychologist, the chaplain, was now a clean-up guy? He noticed the confusion on my face.

"Whatever is my task, I do my best," he explained. "I couldn't talk, how could I counsel people? I needed to be useful and contribute to the community, so I did what I could do, working with my hands. In the military, I was also trained to be an electrician, but we don't have any electricity here. I had to do something and be a working member of our society."

"But clean up?" I must have been making a face.

He smiled at me, a comforting smile. "God gives us all kinds of things to do. We don't always have to be doing the most important thing."

I thought about the job I had been doing in the Complex, solving puzzles that I had been told were codes, yet they were merely puzzles that were invented by the Complex administrators to give me a task to do, to keep my busy. All the years I lived and worked there, I thought I was one of the elite, walking around feeling like I was so important, more important than the people who cooked our food and managed our hair and cleaned up after us. I actually was never doing the important thing.

As it turned out, all that time, the important thing was right here, clear across on the other side of the world: my dad and the life he was living. Now it was so obvious to me that my old technologically enhanced, controlled life was a farce, and this simple life of interacting with people, people helping each other so they all could survive, was a genuine life of true significance. I could already see that this culture allowed people to show their feelings. They had feelings! They weren't required to oppress them until they forgot what feelings were.

So what if my dad was a clean-up guy? He was part of a community, a helpful and functioning society, and he did a job he was capable of doing without using his voice.

"Now that you can talk again, are you still going to clean up?" It was a miracle that he could talk, after years of silence, when we found each other again.

"I haven't thought much about it. All I can think about is you."

He made me feel so warm in my heart, I almost felt like I was going to cry again. The best part was, I was allowed to cry. That fact alone made me not need to cry. I gave Dad a big smile and stood up to hug him. I was prepared to stay here forever with him and become a clean-up person alongside him.

"I'll help you," I said eagerly.

"I'm sure your help will be much appreciated by everyone here," he said. "I suppose I should start introducing you to the others, although I suspect the word has already spread that you are my daughter."

"Where are the kids?" I asked. He had mentioned eighteen men in the community, and I had seen most of them when we went to get our food, but I hadn't seen the six kids yet.

"Oh, you will get to meet them," Dad assured me. "They have gone on a hunting and gathering trip with a couple of the men and they will be back this afternoon. There are two girls and four boys, and they are all just about your age, maybe a little younger."

"I guess they all speak Arabic?"

"Yes, but now we can help them with their English. They learned it back when they were in school but they haven't had much of a chance to use it. I have heard them speaking English a bit among themselves when I think they were trying to keep secrets from the men."

"Secrets?" I asked. In a community of twenty-four people, how could anyone have a secret?

"Secrets of the young," he said mischievously. "You know, this boy likes this girl and this boy wants to kiss this girl, things like that. Apparently, if they did know I could understand English, they were confident that I wouldn't tell their fathers."

When I heard the phrase "tell their fathers," a pang of jealousy went through me. Even though I was now with my own father, all the years we had spent apart still hurt, and these kids had been with their fathers for the past nine years.

"In the culture where they lived before the bombings, or The Great Devastation, as you call it, couples often got married as teenagers," he explained, "but since we have only two girls and four boys, they decided to wait, so they could make their own decisions. Two of the boys are brothers, and their father is not with us, so they were adopted, in a sense, by two of the men, so each child would have a father, one person to look out for each of them. But we have all been family to each other. I imagine you will be like a distant cousin to them, a cousin they have not yet met."

"Cousin?" I asked excitedly. I had never had a cousin before, or even anyone resembling a cousin. Strangers were to become like family to me, and this was a most thrilling feeling.

"Are you finished eating?" my dad asked.

I had been so very hungry, but my plate was still nearly full.

"I don't think so," I said, looking at the huge amount of food I had brought to the table.

"Take your time."

"It's just that so much —" I began. I couldn't finish the sentence, it was just so much of everything: food on my plate, ideas in my head, people in my new family, feelings in my heart. At the Complex, the whole idea of families was completely rejected. How had I existed without being part of a family all those years? Oh, yes, I had merely existed; I hadn't been really living because part of my being, the feeling part, had been deactivated. Now that it was reactivated, I suspected that I was going to have a 'feelings overload' very soon.

"I know exactly what you mean," he said knowingly, and I was sure his statement was completely accurate, even though our living situations for the past nine years had been complete opposites.

I took another bite of the roasted meat, oh, so delicious, and decided not to ask what type of meat it was. If my dad told me it was rabbit or chipmunk or gopher, or any unusual critter (it was not chicken or turkey), I wouldn't be able to eat it with the image of one of those cute little animals in my mind. I was satisfied just knowing that if this foreign meat was good enough for my dad to eat, it was good enough for me, whatever it was.

A man peeked his head in the fold of the hut.

"*Marhaba*," he said. He looked from my dad to me and back to my dad, as if he didn't believe his eyes.

From way back in my memory, I knew he was giving

us a type of greeting, somewhat of a "hello."

"*Marhaba,*" my dad said to him.

The man looked astonished and began to speak rapidly in Arabic as he stepped inside the hut. The only word I caught was the word for 'father,' which he pronounced in an unfamiliar way, but I guessed he was discussing the fact that my dad was my dad and I was his daughter. I thought the man was also caught off guard when my dad spoke to him, after nine years of silence.

"*Ingleezi*?" I asked, on the off chance that he may know some English.

"Ingleesh?" he said, his eyes widening. "You Ingleesh?"

"I speak English," I said, nodding. This was a very handsome man with dark features and surprisingly beautiful, almond-shaped green eyes. Suddenly I was afraid that maybe children weren't allowed to speak to adults, and I looked quickly at my dad for confirmation or permission. Dad said something to the man which included my name, probably an introduction.

"This is Sameer," Dad said to me.

"Nice to meet you," I said, and Dad translated for me. I needed to remember my languages, but those words I had learned so long ago were buried too far beneath the surface of my mind. Two phrases were there: 'I love you' and 'I want some water,' but neither of those were to be used at this time. However, I had no doubt that it would come back to me quickly, as I was now immersed in a community where this language was spoken all the time.

"Sameer has a son," Dad said, "and he is also named

Sameer. In their culture, the first born son is always named after his father, so you will learn that we have several duplicate names here." The thought entered my mind that in a community of only 24 people, they didn't need to duplicate names, but since they had been named before the population reduction, it wouldn't have made sense to change their names. Dad spoke rapidly to Sameer and I figured that he was translating what he had just told me.

Sameer nodded at me and smiled, revealing straight, white teeth. I began to hope that his son would be as nice looking as he was, and that he would be very near my age. He said something else to my dad, then he bowed his head slightly as he backed to the door, or, rather, the flap.

"Gute-bye," he said to me, with a smile. "*Asalaamo alikum.*"

"*Wi alikum isalaam,*" my dad said, as my mind brought up "peace be with you;" "and upon you, peace." Maybe my Arabic language phrases would come back quickly, in spurts.

"I have to brush up on my Arabic," I told Dad, after Sameer left.

"I'm sure you will have no trouble at all with it," Dad assured me. "You will get a lot of practice."

"How much?" I asked, teasing.

"A LOT!" Dad said, laughing, as we both recalled one of the jokes we used so long ago. When someone would use the phrase 'a lot,' one of us would ask, 'how much?' in an attempt to point out how vague that expression was.

"Where do you get your water?" I asked, a question

that had been in the back of my mind.

"We have a well, not too far from here. And there's another well within walking distance, so we have plenty of water for all of us."

"Ah, that's good."

"We couldn't stay here if we didn't have a source of water. But I suppose that is obvious." He moved over to a chair that was made of some kind of wood and possibly animal hair. "We have everything we need to survive here."

"Are you going to stay here forever?"

"I cannot tell what the future will bring, but as a group, we are planning to stay here as long as we can. Now that you are here, I am not so sure how long I will stay here. Now that I know people are alive in other parts of the world, maybe we can go to where they are." He shrugged his shoulders a couple of times, his way of kind of throwing an idea up in the air.

"No!" I almost shouted. "I mean, we don't want to go back to the Complex, not ever. I didn't realize it when I lived there, but now I am sure it is an evil place. They would not even let us worship God and they did not allow families to be together. We were all just cogs in their idea of some wheel that was turning for no reason. We had no freedom."

"We do have freedom here, but we don't have all the things you had there, and you look like you turned out all right."

I looked him right in the eye, right in his loving, brown eyes, that looked just like mine. "I turned out all right because of how you raised me, you and Mom. No matter where I could have lived, I had a good foundation that you taught me."

He smiled. "We don't have to go back to where you lived," he said. "We can go and try to find your mother."

"Mom?" I asked, shocked. That was about the last thing I expected to hear him say. My heart seemed to swell in my chest.

"Why not? You found me. The two of us together, with God, can do more than we can imagine. We can do great things, including finding someone we really love."

"How could we find her?" I asked, shaking my head. "Can we just start walking across the desert, all over the world, until we find her?"

"I don't know yet, but now that I know you are alive, I have a very strong feeling that she is also still alive. I always felt you were both alive, but I had just accepted the facts when everyone at the Four Quadrants had died."

I leaned back on the bench so I was supported by the table as my body went a little bit limp. Perhaps my mind had been so conditioned by the State, by the rulers at the Complex, that my imagination was stagnant. Before I found my dad, I thought he had died, and I had been wrong about that. The possibility existed that my mother was still alive, and out there somewhere, on the Outside. They had snatched me away from her for a reason, a reason I did not understand, but what had they done with her? She hadn't been sick, I was positive of that. Their attempts to make me think she was in one of those hospitals or homes worked while I was under their influence, but now I was free from them and their manipulations. My mind was now liberated, able to imagine that she was alive, and I began at that moment to believe that Daddy and I could find her, with God's help. What an exciting thought! Our family could be reunited, after all this time!

"I need to go to a meeting," my dad said, "so you can just relax here for awhile. My Bible is over there, if you want to do some reading while you wait." He motioned to a little stack of things in the corner.

"A meeting?" I looked at him anxiously.

"Now that you are here, we know we are not the only civilization left on earth. We have some things to discuss," he said, placing his hand on my shoulder.

"I guess this is the first time you will be able to participate in a meeting since you joined these guys."

"Yes, it is," he said thoughtfully. I saw a look flash across his face that somehow caused me to feel a little bit worried. What if they didn't want us to stay with them, since I was an outsider? Or worse, what if they wanted me to marry one of the boys so their little clan could be grow to be a little bit bigger? In the Bible, Jacob's family of 72 souls, as I recalled, grew to be millions of people by the time Moses became their leader.

I took a deep breath and realized that these people were nice and loving, and that they had accepted my dad into their clan. I had to stop thinking Complex thoughts, paranoid thoughts, thoughts of evil and not good. It was time to do some searching of the Scriptures, and I stood up to go get the Bible.

"Some water is over there, in those bottles, and I won't be gone long, I promise," my dad said.

For a second, I felt like I was going to panic. I didn't want my dad to leave me! We just found each other, after being apart for too many years.

"Can I go with you, to the meeting?" I asked, holding

the Bible in both hands.

"Children don't go to the meetings," he stated. His face softened and he smiled. "But you are not really a child any more, are you?"

I did feel like a child, especially around my dad, but I was seventeen years old, which is practically an adult in some cultures, or used to be, anyway. Wasn't King Tut only thirteen when he was king?

"You won't understand much, but I can explain everything we talk about after the meeting."

"It doesn't matter if I don't understand, I just want to be there with you." I could not bear to be parted from him, even for a short time.

"I want you with me as well," he said, standing up to give me a hug. "Yes, it's much better for you to come with me, so you won't disappear while I'm gone, and then I will discover you have been only a figment of my imagination."

"Seeing is believing!" I said, hugging him tightly.

"Squeezing is believing, too," he said, in the funny voice of a person being squished.

CHAPTER 2

The men spoke so rapidly while we were in the meeting, I could not understand even one word. We were in a large hut, much larger than my dad's hut, where they had a large round table with benches and stools all around it. I was sitting beside my dad, and since I had no idea what they were discussing, I looked from one man to another to get an idea of who my new neighbors were. Inside the hut, they removed their hoods and I could get a good look at their faces. I recognized the man I first met when I arrived, the one who had led me to my dad, and beside my dad, on the other side of him, sat Sameer. All had dark brown or black hair and they were all very handsome. Only one man had blue eyes, two had green eyes, and the rest had brown eyes. My dad looked a lot like everyone else, but he was the best-looking man in the hut, by far. His eyes were the most kind, his expression was the most relaxed.

The discussion seemed to be extremely heated, where no one was allowed to finish a sentence before being interrupted, usually by two men who were sitting across the table from us. Those two guys seemed to be angry, and one guy seemed to be always trying to get them to be calm. I felt so out of touch, almost like watching a movie with no sound and trying to guess what they were saying — except they were so loud.

Before the meeting ended and before they could come to some kind of agreement or resolution, the sound of shouting and laughter came from a distance. The assembly stopped the discussion and everyone ran out of the hut.

"What's happening?" I asked my dad.

"The children are returning from the hunt," he said, as we followed the others.

I could hear children's voices, cheerful and loud, excited and proud, as the group approached us. They were wearing robes with hoods, and I guessed it was to protect them from the extreme heat. They were animated, lively, talking and laughing among themselves, and I got a good feeling from them. I was looking forward to being welcomed by them, to be one of the 'cousins' in their family.

Suddenly they all stopped in their tracks, frozen like statues, and they were all silent and staring — right at me. The air was hot and thick, and I felt as if I were the one who should do or say something, but I couldn't move. My mouth was sealed. I was the stranger, I was the object of their scrutiny. I wanted to disappear, or I wanted someone to make me feel welcome, or please, anyone, just say something!

The children looked to be about my age, with the exception of one boy who looked a lot younger. The girls were so beautiful, with their enormous dark eyes and full, red lips. The boys were all so cute, I was embarrassed to look directly at them, like I was invading 'adorable' land. I instantly knew which boy was Sameer's son — he looked like a younger version of his father, his features just the same, only not as refined as his father's.

I forced myself to look at the ground in front of me, not wanting to appear rude and staring and them, even though that is exactly what they were doing to me. Days seemed to pass before the silence was broken.

"Ingleesh?" one of the boys said. "You are of Ingleesh?"

"I-I-I s-speak English," I stammered, afraid to raise my gaze to the group.

"This is my daughter," my dad said proudly, in English. At this, I was able to hold up my head and look at them again.

"You daughter?" one boy said, as they all moved a little closer to us. "How she get here? You hiding her a long time?"

One of the men said something rapidly in Arabic, and the kids nodded with understanding. I assumed the man was explaining my arrival, but for all I knew, he could have been telling them I had just sprung up in the desert like a cactus. I smiled shyly, hoping to be accepted. After all, I was becoming part of this community. I was probably going to be living here for a long time with them, and I wanted them to like me. I wanted — no, I needed — some new friends.

"Where you from?" Sameer's son asked, his voice smooth and delicate.

"How you far walk here?" another boy asked. His English was heavily tinted with an Arabic sound to it.

The tallest boy, the cutest boy, took a step towards me, looked right in my eyes and asked in perfect English, "What is your name?"

"Layla," I answered.

"You Arabic name?" one girl asked critically.

"I don't know," I said defensively. I had never thought about the origins of my name. I looked to my dad, but he was just watching the scene unfold, not participating in this encounter of the teenagers.

The cute boy who had asked my name said, "My

name is Nadir. It is very nice to meet you, Layla." He reached over and gently lifted my hand to his lips. I felt a little tingly and a lot embarrassed, and the other kids all laughed. I looked up at my dad, and he was just smiling.

"Sameer, but you can call me Sammy," Sameer's son said, stepping over to me.

"I am Jamal," the other boy about my age said, giving his head a firm nod.

"Essom," the youngest boy said, waving, remaining a distance away from me.

The boys looked to the girls, waiting for them to introduce themselves. I was hoping they were shy and not shunning me; or maybe it was just their custom to let the boys speak first?

"I am Lena," the girl who had criticized my name said, her voice softening. "I have before a sister named Layla." Her eyes clouded over and I knew she had lost someone she loved.

"I'm sorry," I said.

"Why you are sorry?" Essom asked, tilting his head a little. "You did nothing to her sister."

"We say, 'I'm sorry' to express sympathy," I explained.

"Yes," Essom said, nodding.

"My name is Salwa," the other girl said, very quietly, giving me a shy smile. I figured she was a little younger than I was, but Lena was probably just about my age.

"You speak English very well," I told them.

"We practice every day," Jamal said, giving me a look that made me feel just a bit creepy. That was definitely not the look a boy gives to his cousin. He grinned at me impishly.

As we stood in the heat of the day, I wondered if anyone else felt like they were burning up, from both inside and outside. I didn't have on a hood, but still, they must have felt the rising temperature.

I turned to my dad. "I need a glass of water," I said.

"I don't have a glass, but I have some water," he replied, smiling at me. "Come on." He walked toward his hut and I followed him, leaving the group of kids behind us.

I heard the sound of steps thumping on the sand and suddenly Jamal was beside me.

"Your clothing," he said. "How you make it?" He began to reach for my shirt, then withdrew his hand.

"I didn't make it. This is what I wear," I said, a feeble explanation.

"You make some like this for me?" he asked.

"And for all of us," Sameer added, and I realized the entire group was crowding around me.

"I don't know how to make clothes," I said, as it dawned on me that I didn't really know how to do anything that would count for a survival skill out here in the desert. Then I remembered something. "I have some clothes that I think Lena and — what's the other girl's name? Salad?"

"Salwa," she corrected quietly.

"I have some clothes that Lena and Salwa can probably wear," I said, recalling the extra clothing in the backpack I had brought when we left the plane, about a hundred years ago; or did that happen only two or three days ago?

"You have clothes for me?" Salwa asked, astonished.

I had been so eager to make my new acquaintances like me, I had not considered the fact that I had only two changes of clothes, besides the ones I was wearing. Then I decided that I would soon be dressing the same way they were, in a robe. They must have extra robes around, or the ability to make them. Maybe I could even learn how to make my own robe, if someone gave me the material and showed me how to do it.

I nodded, with the conviction that I would give to the girls the other outfits I had brought. I had not even taken a good look at them, as they had been vacuum-wrapped in plastic so they only took up a tiny amount of space. That was the way all of our new clothes had been packaged, as far back as I could remember, to keep them fresh and new until someone bought them and opened the package.

"Thank you, I thank you," Lena said, warming up to me. She gave me a very beautiful smile, and I could see her long, dark hair beneath the hood of her robe.

"You have no clothes for me?" Nadir asked, moving close to me.

"I didn't know you were here," I said defensively.

"We want this clothes," he informed me.

A thought occurred to me, but I needed to ask my dad about it privately before suggesting it. Besides, were they even allowed to wear any different clothes besides robes? Maybe it was a cultural thing and perhaps I had overstepped my boundaries as a newcomer by offering to dress the girls in regular clothes.

"I need to go inside now," I said, leading my dad into

his hut. The heat was roasting the top of my head, and dealing with these kids was making me a little dizzy. Too much was happening in the heat, and I didn't want to act crazy or appear to be a fool in front of people that I wanted to be my friends.

My dad stepped into the hut behind me, and I motioned to him to close the flap before anyone else followed him. He closed it, then he got some water for me in a clay cup. I thanked him and drank it quickly.

"Daddy?" I said tentatively. I could hear the others move away from the hut, so I felt like we had some privacy now.

"Yes, my darling daughter?" he asked.

"I was just thinking," I began.

"Oh, there you go, thinking again," he teased. "You know what happens when you start thinking."

"Yeah, I get ideas." We had this part of this conversation when I was only seven years old.

"And those ideas usually include some grand plan, am I right?"

"Well, I don't know if it's really a grand plan…" I sat on one of the stools, wondering if my idea might actually be possible.

"Does it include doing something complicated, laborious or strenuous?" He gave me that wonderful Daddy smile.

"Not really. Maybe. Yes, I think so."

"Which one?"

"Which one what?" I shook my head, unsure what he meant.

"Will it be complicated, laborious or strenuous?"

"Oh, I don't know, but here it is." I took a deep breath, wondering where to start. "You know when you told me about getting the water and food from the Four Quadrants?"

"Yes, I do recall telling you about that." He sat in his chair, facing me.

"Was it a long time ago? I mean, last time you did that?"

"Why? Do you want more food and water?" He leaned forward in the chair, as if he were about to get some food and water for me.

"No, I was just thinking…"

He relaxed in the chair and smiled. "Yes, of course you were thinking. If I know one thing about you, you are often thinking, and you always have been quite a thinker."

"You said you came across a huge supply of food and water in the mall area—"

"And you think we can go back there, dig through the rubble and find clothes for your friends?"

"Yes! That's exactly what I was thinking!" How did he know? Had he learned to be a mind reader, or was my idea that obvious? More likely, he just knew how I thought, the way my mind worked. Even after we had been apart for nearly nine years, he knew me the way a father should know his daughter, and I loved it. I had missed him so much while we were living on opposite sides of the world! "Can we do that? Can we go to the Mall Quadrant and get clothes for all the kids here?"

"I am not saying it would be impossible," he began,

putting the tips of his fingers on both hands together, the way he did when he was thinking up a plan, "but it would be a lot of work. We haven't been digging in that area for a couple of years, so everything is pretty deeply buried by the sand that blows across that area."

"What else do the kids have to do?" I asked, assuming they must have had plenty of free time to go 'shopping' for clothes that were more fashionable and practical than robes. If we could dig down to where the clothing shops had been in the Mall Quadrant, we would be able to find hundreds of outfits in perfect condition — vacuum sealed and ready to be worn.

"Everyone has his own duties and assignments, things that need to be done every day, but you might have something there. It wouldn't have to be only for the kids. The men could also find some regular clothes to wear, if we make it a team effort. We have not ever discussed our clothing situation but maybe some of the other men would like to have the option of not wearing a robe all the time. I know I would like it. The uniform I was wearing when I found this tribe was pretty well disintegrated by that time and they provided a set of robes for me to wear. I am all for changing into another outfit and wearing pants again. I don't need a lot of clothes, but I wouldn't mind having some other choices."

"I can't believe you never thought of this before," I said, taking another drink of water. All this thinking and planning was making me very thirsty.

"I suppose it takes a female to think about things like fashion," he said. "We have been more focused on surviving." He also took a drink of water.

"Can we start tomorrow?" I asked eagerly. I liked to get into action as soon as an idea was hatched. In addition, the notion of a new wardrobe was beginning to grow on me. We could each get several new outfits and there would still be plenty for everybody. This life in the desert didn't have to be drab and monotonous, not when we had access to free clothing, just over the next hill.

"Hold your horses, my darling daughter," my dad said, miming the action of pulling on the reins of a horse, something he had often done during our life before The Great Devastation. "We have to meet with the elders and make a decision."

"You have to have a meeting to decide if we can go shopping? Well, it would be kind of like shopping."

"It will be a lot of work," my dad said with a sigh. "We would have to go in the early morning, before the day gets too hot. We would have to dig through the sand and go quite deep. I'm not sure of the exact spot we would be searching, since everything was pretty well messed up by the bombings. We have only two or three shovels, and I don't know how many people they would let join in this venture, since some need to stay behind and keep things going here."

"Keep things going here?" I asked. "What kinds of things are going on here?"

My dad seemed to clam up a bit as he shifted in his chair. "The meals, our basic survival, keeping things together, things like that."

He wasn't telling me everything, but I didn't want to get off the subject. I didn't really care what the big adult secrets were in this society. I just wanted to know about our quest for clothing. I had another idea.

"Maybe we can find some shovels there! Then we

can get enough for each of us to use one, and maybe some other equipment, too."

"We would have to dig deep by hand to get to the shovels," my dad reminded me. "But maybe, besides clothing, we can go and dig for other things. We only searched for food before, but we could look for all kinds of things to make our lives better."

"Why didn't you set up the camp, these huts, or tents, or whatever they are, why didn't you set up in the Four Quadrants? Then you would be close to all kinds of resources."

He shook his head and looked at the ground. "I couldn't do it, back then. As soon as I had the opportunity, I had to get away from the place that took away my family, everyone I loved. The only thing I took with me, the only item worth taking away from there, was my Bible, this Bible right here." He lifted it up to make his point. "This, the Word of God, is what has sustained me from the time I lost you and your mother until today."

I nodded. I understood. I would not have wanted to stay in the place where I believed that my loved ones had been killed. My life at the Complex had been so easy — and so far removed from our home — compared with my dad's life since we were separated, all that time he was struggling to survive in the desert.

"So, how long do you think it will take?"

"To convince the others to help with this little project? Actually, we have two options. You and I could go any time, without having to ask permission. We would, of course, tell them where we were going and what we were planning to do, but you and I could go as early as tomorrow morning."

"Let's do it!" I said enthusiastically.

"Or, we can discuss it with the group, and wait a couple of days and have a large crew go with us. Just the two of us, even working hard, wouldn't be able to get much done before we were stopped by the heat of the day. More hands working would give us much faster results. Plus, there is safety in numbers. No, I don't think we should go alone. If anything happened, we would be too far away from here to get help."

"Yeah, you are right," I said, "as usual. We want more help and we want to be safe. One thing they were always drilling into us at the Complex was that we needed, above all, at all times, to be safe."

"Good thinking," he agreed. "I will bring up the idea this evening, when we gather for dinner. Right now, why don't you get a little rest? It is too hot to do anything outside, so we can just stay in here and relax."

"Daddy?" I said, wanting him to do something for me he had not been able to do in years. "Can you read a chapter from the Bible while we are relaxing?"

"Of course, my darling daughter," he agreed. He opened his Bible to one of my favorite chapters, the book of John, chapter 14, and began to read to me the familiar words of Jesus, words that I had not heard in nearly a decade.

"Let not your heart be troubled, you believe in God, believe also in me."

Then I could really relax.

CHAPTER 3

After we ate dinner and everyone was gathered in the largest of the huts, my dad announced that he had a topic of discussion. He decided to speak in English and Nadir offered to translate so the elders (the men) could understand.

"You have all met or seen my daughter, Layla," he began, and most people nodded. "She has come to us by a miracle of God, from the other side of the world, where a functioning technological society is living. She has reported there are many people living in the Complex, where she lived, as well as others who are living in other communities."

This statement brought some murmuring and low discussion, and from the expressions on their faces, I thought some of them had been suspecting they were not the only people left on the face of the earth. My dad waited until they were quiet again before he continued.

"We have no reason to leave our community here and try to find anyone else. They came by airplane and helicopter and the others who came with my daughter don't know of our existence here.

"However, you all see that my daughter is dressed differently than we are. Our other children have expressed that they would like to dress in a similar manner."

Again, much discussion, this time a little louder, and possibly protesting.

"It is true!" Nadir shouted in English. "The robes may be satisfactory for you, but they are not for us. We want to wear pants, like Layla."

"It is not for girl to wear pants," one of the men said, to my surprise, in crude English. "Girl wear dress." His face was so stern, I was a little bit afraid of him.

"*Baba*!" Lena protested. "I want to wear pants."

"Pants for boys, for men!" he insisted.

"Pants are for everyone, girls and boys," Lena argued.

Salwa nodded in agreement. I didn't want to get into the argument, but I also didn't want to be stuck always wearing a dress, or worse, one of those bulky robes.

"We can get more clothes!" I said loudly, immediately regretting that I had spoken.

The kids started chattering in both English and Arabic, and the elders, with their low voices, were speaking at the same time. After about a minute of this confusing rumble, my dad whistled loudly, a talent I had forgotten he had. The hut was instantly silent.

"We know where there is a large supply of clothes," my dad said, "not just for the children, but for all of us. You don't have to change your way of dress or put aside your robe, but I would like some options. This robe is not my preferred outfit of choice. I am confident that we can also find some dresses for the girls."

"Dress and pants?" Lena gasped, turning to her father and clutching onto his arm. "Please, *Baba*! I will wear dress for you and pants for gathering and hunting."

Her father's eyes softened as he looked at his daughter. "Where these clothes?"

"Back at the Four Quadrants, where we were getting

the food and water before," my dad said. "By now, everything is pretty well buried in the sand, but we can dig it out, if we work together. I have a good idea where the clothes are, so we can focus on that area."

"They will be full of sand, bugs eat them," Jamal said, discouraged.

"No, they are in plastic!" I said excitedly. "Vacuum-sealed and as good as new."

"Vacuum-sealed?" Nadir asked, as he was translating my statement.

"Wrapped up in plastic with the air removed, sealed so nothing can get in," I explained. Then I decided I should let my dad do the talking, but I was just so eager to get started, I had to work to contain myself. I was a newcomer, a stranger, a child, and I was in no position to be addressing the elders.

Nadir nodded his head to me, indicating he understood the concept, and translated for me.

The elders looked at me. The children looked at me. I looked at my dad, who smiled at me and put me at ease. I wanted somebody to say something, but they fell silent for a few minutes. I thought they must be considering the situation. I didn't see a down side to my idea, so I had no idea why they were all being so quiet.

One of the elders spoke and Nadir translated for me.

"Sayeed say, it very hot and we have only two — how do you say, for digging?"

"Shovels," my dad said.

"Yes, shoffles, we have just two. The sand very deep and the wind very strong in this place you go. Is worth risking life for this things?" Nadir said, then he answered Sayeed. "We find other things we use for digging. A group go before sun, and dig and look, come back early, before heat and go back next day, early. We do this until we find clothes for all. Children go every day and some men go, some stay."

"Other people?" Sameer Senior asked, in English. "Other people at this place?"

I began to realize most of them knew some English but had no reason to use it since The Great Devastation.

"No, no one is there," my dad assured him.

"You daughter come from this place?" Sameer asked.

"No, she was living far away from there and just happened to come through there with some friends."

"They kill us or capture us," Sameer insisted. He looked frightened.

"They are gone, no one is there," my dad explained. "They left her there and she came here."

"Why she come here, to us?" Sameer asked suspiciously.

"I don't know why I came here," I said. "I guess I was directed by God, so I could find my dad. My friends went back to the plane and I walked here, but I didn't know why I was coming this way, I just walked, and I found you." It still seemed unreal to me, and I had done it. I was sure what I was saying sounded unbelievable.

"Let us vote," Nadir suggested.

"Nadir!" a man shouted firmly. "You are not elder and this no democracy."

"Yes, *Baba*," Nadir said submissively. I suspected this was Nadir's father. They did look alike, both very handsome, but then, this little community had a monopoly on good-looking males.

One of the elders suggested something and Nadir translated for me. "A show of hands if you want to go dig and search the ruins."

Ouch; it hurt me to hear our former home, the Four Quadrants, being called 'ruins,' but that's exactly what had become of our city.

About half the men and all of the children raised their hands. As the kids looked around at the response, they cheered.

"We will go!" Sammy said.

"When we will go?" Lena asked.

"Start in morning?" Nadir suggested. "Early, before sun we start."

The group agreed that we would walk to the Four Quadrants — or, actually, the ruins of the Four Quadrants — the next morning, and start digging to find clothing and perhaps other items we could use.

CHAPTER 4

In the middle of the night I was awakened by all kinds of noises and talking. I struggled to get my bearings in the darkness.

"Layla," my dad said, coming into the hut carrying a lantern, "wake up. We will be leaving in a few minutes."

My internal clock was telling me that it was not any time near morning, but I pulled myself out from the light blanket I was using and sat on the mat.

Dad was holding a cloth out to me. "Here is a damp rag for you to wash your face."

I wiped my face, rubbed my eyes, and forced myself to be ready to get going immediately. We were starting on an adventure!

Before I was completely awake, about a dozen of us were walking through the cool desert in the dark. I had no idea what time it was, but it didn't really matter. My dad and some of the others were carrying lanterns, and I had on my back a pack full of bottles of water. I tried to not look directly at the flames in the lanterns, because they turned to glowing balls in my vision and I was unable to see anything else. I forced myself to keep my eyes on my dad's back, to follow his footsteps across the sand. I wasn't alert enough to follow any of the conversation floating about me; it was all I could do to just walk, step by step, without any bearings or landmarks in sight.

Suddenly I felt a warmth against my skin, a touch on my shoulder, and I jumped. I was immediately wide awake.

"Do not be afraid," a male voice whispered in my

ear. I could feel his hot breath on my neck. "You are so beautiful, precious one."

I turned to see who was the owner of this voice, but I could only see the outline of the hooded robe in the dim light of the lanterns.

"I want you to be my own," he whispered. Before I could say anything, or even think of anything, he blended in with the other hooded figures which were escorting me.

I was so glad it was dark, because I knew I was blushing. My face felt hot, and suddenly my clothing was smothering me. I wondered who had been speaking to me, saying intimate things so quietly to me, and I hoped it had been Sammy, Nadir or Jamal, and not one of the fathers. The only guy I could rule out for sure was Essom, because he wasn't tall enough to whisper in my ear.

As I was considering the person who whispered to me, trying to decide which one it was, another voice whispered in my other ear.

"You are sent to me," he said softly. "You will love me."

I quickly turned my head so I could see the face of the person secretly speaking to me, but he stepped back into the group before I could see who he was.

We kept walking. The morning was so dark, I wondered how anyone could guide us to our destination. I kept my eyes on my dad's back and hoped I wouldn't get another whisper in my ear. Gradually the atmosphere began to lighten — literally, before the sun came up. As I examined our surroundings, I still could not see how we could be sure we were going in the right direction. There were no hills, no roads, no landmarks: there was nothing but flat sand everywhere I could see. Without the sun having risen yet, it was almost impossible to tell which direction was east — as if that would make a difference to me.

Then it dawned upon me that it did make a difference to me. When I left the Four Quadrants that day and walked to where my dad was, where the group of huts was, I somehow knew I was walking southeast. So now the sun should be rising behind us. As I looked closely at the sky, I could see that it was a little darker straight ahead of us and it was a little lighter directly behind us. I felt like I was somehow a little bit in control, because I now was sure we were going in the right direction.

Although there were no hills that I could see, I became aware that we were walking up a slight incline. Yes, this seemed familiar, because on my excursion across the desert the other day, I was, for the most part, going slightly downhill. We had to be getting close to the ruins of the Four Quadrants: we had been walking for quite some time. I wasn't getting tired, but I was certainly getting anxious to arrive so we could start on our task.

The thought occurred to me that this was the most time I had spent Outside in years. At the Complex, we had our daily mandatory outdoor time, but being out in the desert, outside of an air-conditioned structure for this length of time was certainly revitalizing me. All this fresh air I was inhaling seemed to be giving me super-charged blood. I felt as if I could keep walking for days — except I could feel the stress in the muscles of my legs, the slight cramping in my calves.

One step after another, one, two, one, two, and

I nearly bumped into my dad when he stopped. The group spread out, left to right, and I saw that we were standing on the ridge of the valley where the Four Quadrants had once been, the ridge where I had stood when I decided to walk into the desert just a few days ago. Ahead of us was the memorial area where my dad had set up all the crosses, and beyond that was the faintest resemblance of the crossroads. Maybe I could only see the remains of the roads because I knew where they had been, but no matter. My dad took the lead as we made our way to the where the Mall Quadrant had once stood.

Going down the incline into the valley was much easier than going up had been, but my legs did not want to cooperate with the urgency I was feeling. Some muscles in my thighs I guess I had never used before were begging me to stop, to sit and rest. Had we been going uphill for two or three hours? My skater's muscles were not the same ones used as a climber's muscles, but I didn't want to ask to stop or seem like a whiner. If the others could make it without complaining, so could I; but it did cross my mind that I would love to put on my roller skates and glide down the hill to the Mall Quadrant.

As we passed the field of crosses, my dad stopped.

"Let us stop for a moment and take a drink of water," he said hoarsely, as he pulled a bottle of water out of his pack.

I swallowed and noticed that my throat was extremely dry. I pulled out a bottle of water and took a drink, and I could feel the moisture going to every part of my body. I wanted to quickly drink the entire bottle of water, but I knew that wasn't the best idea. I did gulp down half of it without even taking a breath. I was so thankful to be giving my aching muscles a short rest. I squatted on the ground, to stretch my muscles in a different direction and took a few deep breaths.

"You are okay?"

I looked up to see Nadir leaning over me. I nodded.

"You are tired?" he asked, concern in his eyes.

"I am okay," I said. I didn't know how to express what a great adventure this was for me, to be outside the Complex for such a long time and to be doing a physical activity that was lasting so long, needing my endurance. This exciting voyage to me was most likely just an everyday kind of happening for these kids. They were always outside, going hunting (which seemed kind of awful to me) and gathering food and exploring, so they would not be able to understand what a Complex-dweller, a person who spent ninety-five percent of her time indoors, was feeling right now. In my mind, I was so excited, but I was pushing my body to its limits.

He put out his hand to help me stand up again. As I took it, I was surprised at how soft it was. I was expecting it to be rough or hard, but it was smooth and soft. He pulled me up easily, and I noticed how strong he was. He gave a little tug just as I was completely upright, causing me to be thrown off balance and fall against him. I saw the mischievous look on his face as he put both his hands gently on my upper arms and slowly pushed me away from him.

I was completely embarrassed and I hoped no one else had seen his little trick. He must have been one of the whisperers earlier; I felt a warm rush inside me as I was pretty sure he might be flirting with me. He was so tall, so good-looking, and he seemed to be very nice. While I was not ready to commit myself to one of these guys whom I had so recently met, he definitely was worth considering; but maybe later, after we could get to know each other.

"I am okay," I repeated, looking for my dad, who had moved away from me. I could not just stand there and look straight at a handsome guy who was smiling at me. I saw my dad was putting away his water bottle and I stepped over to be close to him.

"Are you about ready?" he asked me quietly.

"Yes, I am ready," a little more enthusiastically than I should have, trying to cover up my bit of nervousness. "Let's go!"

"*Yalla,*" my dad said loudly. Everyone got ready to go, and my dad said to me, "Let's go."

We started moving, and I had a good feeling to be so near to the Mall Quadrant, or where it once stood. We didn't have far to go now. I stayed close to my dad, walking beside him so I would not be walking beside any of the other guys. I was having enough of a problem feeling like the outsider in the group, and I didn't want to get into a conversation with any of these guys at this time. The excitement was evident in the increased volume of the chatter around me, which was growing more animated the closer we got to our target.

My dad stopped a little sooner than I thought he should have. I felt that the Mall Quadrant was further, maybe another half mile away from where we stood.

"Let us start here," he said, pointing to an area in front of him. "If we spread out, we can cover this section. "I suggest we work in pairs or three together. The two with the shovels, start digging on the outer edges, over there and there, while the rest of us dig with our hands, or anything else you brought to use to dig."

He saw the puzzled look on my face.

"Wasn't the Mall Quadrant more over there, down that way?" I asked, pointing in that direction.

"We are actually very close to where it stood," my dad said. "However, things were quite shifted after the bombings. And remember, you were a lot younger, smaller, so things probably seemed larger and farther to you then than they really are."

"That makes sense," I said doubtfully.

"Plus, one other thing, you are probably thinking of the portion of the Mall Quadrant where we did our shopping. We are starting to dig here, in this general area, where the hardware was kept. We will need more shovels and other tools to be able to do the job more efficiently."

I was about to ask why we had to be so efficient, since we had nothing else to do, when I noticed a couple of the men taking supplies from their packs and beginning to set up a tent.

Before I could ask the question, my dad answered. "This job is going to take us at least a few days, and it would not make any sense to walk all the way back to our village. We are going to set up camp here."

"That's a good idea," I agreed. I had been thinking we would just come here, do a little digging, find the treasure, take what we wanted, and go back. Now that we were here and I pictured the structures standing, which were now buried in the sand, I began to think that my idea was going to be a huge undertaking, a nearly impossible task.

I counted the people: seven kids plus eight adults, so, we had a work crew of fifteen people. Naturally, I stayed near my dad, who would be my partner, and we would work side by side.

One of the men shouted something in Arabic and the other two girls went over to him. As he began to speak to them, my dad turned to me.

"You should probably join the girls, over there," he suggested.

"Why? I want to work with you," I protested.

"The girls are going to prepare the meals and do lighter work than the men," he explained quietly.

"But—" I began, then I realized that I was not in any condition to do heavy work right now. As a matter of fact, I was quite tired just from the walk, and the muscles in my legs were aching. As excited as I was to start digging and find something, buried treasures, my body was telling me to take it easy.

"Okay, Daddy," I said, and went over to where the two girls were taking things out of their packs.

"I'm going to work with you," I told them, as they were busy setting things on the ground.

"Work?" Lena asked. "You are going to work?" She pronounced the words carefully and she looked puzzled.

"I am going to help you," I clarified.

Salwa and Lena both looked at me as if they didn't understand what I was saying.

"Cook and stuff," I said, trying to clear up the confusion. "Whatever you guys are doing, I am going to do it with you."

"We not are guys," Salwa said. "We are girls." She kind of rolled her r's, making her sentences sound so fancy.

"It's just an expression," I said, getting a little bit frustrated. Why could I not remember more Arabic so I could communicate with them more clearly? "I will cook with you."

They nodded their heads, finally understanding what I was telling them.

"You build fire," Lena instructed.

I felt so useless. I had no idea how to build a fire, where to build a fire, or what to use to start a fire. I shook my head and shrugged my shoulders, trying to let them know that I wasn't refusing, I just did not know how to get started.

They understood my body language and Lena threw me a look of disappointment; or she almost seemed as if she had expected that type of reaction.

"I'm sorry," I said. "I don't know how to make a fire or how to cook," I confessed.

"You too good to cook?" Lena asked.

"You work like man?" Salwa asked.

"No, no, back home, where I came from, I worked with a computer and solved puzzles," I explained, wondering if they had ever heard of computers.

Their eyes grew wide and they stared at me, four large brown eyes focused on my face.

"Computers?" they both whispered at the same time.

"You have heard of computers?" I asked, lowering my voice, not sure why this must be a secret.

"Yes, but no, how you call it?" Lena said, searching for the right words. "No electric in world after war come and destroy all people and machine. How you use computer?"

"Where I came from, very far from here, there are lots of people and we have electricity, solar power, and we use computers."

"You come from here," Salwa said, pointing at the ground, or perhaps she was asking me about it.

"I did come from here, before the war," I said, since they were not aware of the term 'The Great Devastation.' "Just before the war started, my mother and I got on a plane and we left this area and it was bombed."

"You mother?" Salwa asked, as her eyes grew even wider. "Where she is now, you mother?"

"I don't know where she is," I said, shaking my head sadly. "We were separated shortly after the plane landed in the United States, or what was the United States, back then."

"'Separated shortly?'" Lena asked. "What is this 'separated shortly' you speak?"

"I mean, a short time after the plane landed, we were separated," I said. I realized I was going to have to be more selective with my words and phrases if I didn't want to spend all day explaining what I meant every time I said something.

"Your mother is still alive," Lena said, and I was not sure if she was asking a question or making a statement. My heart leapt.

"I don't know if she is, I mean, I hope she is, but I don't know where she is, I can't be sure."

"You have hope," Salwa said. "Hope is good."

"Yes, you are right. Hope is good." I wanted to be hopeful in this situation, but finding my mother alive did seem nearly impossible. However, Salwa was correct, and my hope was sparked, ever so slightly. After all, I had found my dad, and that had seemed utterly impossible, since all reports had told me he had died in the bombings. At least I knew my mother had not died in the bombings, because we were together at that time, and we both survived.

"We cook and you watch and learn," Lena instructed.

"And just let me know if I can help you," I said.

Lena and Salwa laughed, as if my offer had been ridiculous, so I laughed, too. I wanted so badly to be friends with them, for them to like me.

I glanced back at the men and boys, who were digging and already sweating. The temperature was rising, and I wondered how long into the day they would work before entering the cool of the tents that two of the men had erected.

Lena and Salwa worked swiftly, and although I watched Salwa make a fire, I knew that I would not be able to do it unless she told me, step by step, what she was doing. She dug a small pit then moved some things around and put some things in the pit and took a substance and then the fire was burning. I had not been watching her exclusively, since I was fascinated by the way Lena was making dough out of some substance and water, which she kneaded and separated into the little balls which she flattened between her hands, then slapped onto a large, flat stone and by the time she had some of them laid out, Salwa had the fire ready. Lena expertly placed the flat stone onto stacks of stones Salwa had put inside the pit and Lena went back to the dough. Salwa flipped the flat loaves over after a few minutes and the side that had been down had brown spots on it. The bread smelled so good and I knew it was just about ready to eat. I wondered what other food they were going to fix. I would have been satisfied with just the bread.

Salwa removed the loaves as they got done and wrapped them in a large towel. In the meantime, Lena put the rest of the dough patties onto the stone on the fire. She then removed a large container from a pack and pulled out some onions and some green peppers. She took out a small knife and began cutting them into pieces, which she placed into a large bowl. I was amazed, not only at their cooking skills, but at the efficient way everything had been packed so we would have all these dishes and utensils to use.

Salwa finished cooking the loaves of bread on the fire, and she took a large cup from the pack. As soon as she removed the lid, I could smell garlic, and my stomach began to growl. I figured that sound was universal, and Salwa smiled at me.

"Do you know hummus?" she asked, holding up the container.

"Yes!" I almost shouted. "I love hummus!"

"We eat hummus each morning with bread and vegetables," she explained.

"Do you make fresh bread every day?" I asked, inhaling the heavenly scent.

"I do not make French bread," Lena said.

"No, I mean, do you make bread every day?" I clarified. Obviously, when a person made bread every day it was fresh, I thought, after the statement had been made.

"I do not make bread at camp," Lena said. "The men make all food. When time for gather and hunt, I cook and Salwa cook."

"I see," I said, nodding my head.

"You see what?" Salwa said, looking around to see.

I laughed. "Oh, 'I see' means 'I understand,'" I said, with a little chuckle.

"Why you not say, 'I understand,' if you mean to say you understand?" Lena asked.

"I don't know, they both mean the same thing," I said, shrugging my shoulders.

The girls nodded and went back to their cooking tasks. I was feeling like there was nothing I could do to help, until I remembered my dad and his job. I was able to do something to help! I could help them clean up after we finished eating. For now, though, my task was to learn what they were doing. In the future when we went on treks and adventures, gathering and hunting (could I really hunt? At least I could cook for the hunters, once I learned how to cook), the three of us would be doing this together and I did not want to appear to be useless. Before I knew it, the girls had the food ready.

"*Da-un il-ukl!*" Lena shouted.

By the reaction of the men, who dropped what they were doing and gathered around us, I assumed she called had them to come and eat. I really had a lot to learn. I could not expect them to do all the language learning. I had to at least try to meet them in the middle, if not halfway. I did know some Arabic once, way back in the Time Before, so I had a little bit of a start.

'"*Ukl*' means eat?" I asked, forcing myself to get over my shyness in this area.

"Yes!" Salwa said in a congratulatory manner and smiling at me as if I were a child speaking my first word. Actually, I was grateful for her encouragement.

"What we have to eat?" Nadir asked in English, as he stepped very close to me, invading my personal space. I didn't mind it though, because he was so cute and so nice. Maybe he would be willing to help me learn Arabic, since he seemed to be the one who was the translator.

"*Il-hummus ma il-bussel wi il-filfil al-ahkdar wi il-khubiz*," Lena said.

I felt so proud of myself; I understood the entire sentence! She had said, 'Hummus with onions, green peppers and bread,' and I could understand every word. Of course, I knew the context and I also knew the translation, but it felt good to know what was being said without having to ask for help.

The men and boys sat in a circle on the ground and it occurred to me how infrequently they washed their hands. Back at the Complex, we washed our hands every time we changed activities, and twice before we ate: once when we left our workstation or pod, then again when we arrived at the Eatery. We had been well-trained on the dangers of spreading germs, so we were very careful to keep our hands clean. I probably washed my hands an average of fifteen times per day at the Complex. Since I had arrived here, I had only cleaned them once or twice per day, using the limited amount of water sparingly. I was following the lead of my dad, and he was not getting sick, so I hoped I would not get sick either.

I helped Salwa and Lena distribute the food, which we had wrapped in tiny towels, with hummus spread on the bread. Everyone paused before eating, and looked to my dad.

"*Ham-du-alla,*" he said, and I understood that to mean 'thank God.'

I sat beside him and we all ate in silence. The food tasted so good, and I was glad to have taken part in its preparation, or, at least, to have watched and learned how it had been prepared. Soon, I would be able to help.

The men and boys ate eagerly, and quickly the bread with hummus and vegetables were gone. Each person shook the crumbs from his towel as he stood, handed the towel to Salwa, who was also finished eating, and quickly returned to work.

"Can I help clean up?" I asked, looking around at the already clean area.

"No thing to clean," she said with a smile, as she folded the towels and placed them neatly in a pile on a stone.

"What can I do to help?" I said, not wanting them to think I was helpless.

"We begin to prepare what you call lunch and dinner and move into tent," Lena explained. "Soon sun will be hot for us."

I understood that we would be spending our day, the heat of the day, inside the tents, since it would be too hot to work or even stay out in the blazing sun for more than a short time. It also made sense to do any cooking now, while the air was still relatively cool, since we wouldn't be able to do it later, in the heat.

Salwa handed me some kind of vegetable, perhaps a type of potato, and showed me how to remove the black marks with a knife. She and Lena worked quickly making more bread and preparing some meat, which they put into a pot with water and set it on the fire to boil. When I was finished with the potato-things, Salwa placed them near the fire, around the sides of the flames.

My dad came over to check on me.

"How are you doing?" he asked. Lena and Salwa continued their tasks while I stood up to stretch my legs.

"Fine," I said. "This is very interesting. I have not ever cooked before," I confessed to him.

"Never?" he asked, clearly surprised. Lena and Salwa stopped what they were doing and stared at me.

"At the Complex, we each had our own tasks, and mine was working with the computer and solving puzzles, not cooking," I said, trying to make an excuse for not knowing how to do this basic survival task. "People who have an aptitude for cooking do all the cooking, and the rest of us do our jobs." I attempted to not sound like an elitist, but I was afraid that was exactly what I sounded like. I did not want to appear like I thought I was better than anyone, when, in fact, I probably did not have a single usable survival skill.

"That sounds like a very efficient way to work," my dad said, making me feel less snobbish. "In a way, we do that as well, since Yusef and Ibrahim like to cook, so they do the cooking at home. But, as you no doubt have seen, the girls also have learned to cook and they take care of the food when groups go on their outings and journeys."

"It does make sense, out here, for everyone to know

how to cook," I admitted. "You know how to cook, don't you, Daddy?"

He chuckled. "Of course I know how to cook, and I can even cook out in the desert, here."

"Well, I am going to learn to cook, too," I said, fully committed to this plan.

"Here!" one of the men shouted. "Something is here!"

Lena, Salwa, my dad and I ran over to where the men were digging. Some of them were about ten feet down in a hole they had dug.

"Look!" Nadir said. "Look at this!" He hit a shovel against something that was buried in the sand and we heard a loud clank. He began to dig around the object and three men moved in to help him, one with a shovel and two digging with some sort of flat tool.

"I think it's a concrete slab," my dad said, "possibly a wall or part of a building."

The men continued digging until they had uncovered a huge piece of what looked like a wall. It took nearly all of the men to lift it and move it out of the way. Underneath it were some huge crates.

"What you call 'jackpot' is here!" Nadir shouted up to my dad, who was still standing beside me. Nadir had a look of astonishment on his face, as if he hadn't really expected to find anything, or, at least, nothing important. He and a couple of the others kept digging until they had a crate nearly uncovered.

"What is it?" I asked.

"Lighting!" Nadir shouted, reading from the box. The men began to chatter rapidly in Arabic.

"This lightning?" Jamal asked. "How they get from sky? How they keep in box?"

"No, not lightning, it is lights," Nadir said, as several men hoisted the crate out of the sand where it had been buried for so long.

I could see the words on the crate, but they were in military terms, so I didn't really understand what they meant. I could not see the words that indicated that the box contained lighting.

My dad shouted, "This is great! Solar powered lighting! We can charge these lamps today while we are sleeping, and use them tonight!"

I had not considered the fact that we would be sleeping during the day, but it made perfect sense. First of all, if anyone else was as tired as I was, they would not be able to stay awake once the desert got really hot, and secondly, we now had lighting so they, or we, would be able to work all night.

Two men pulled the giant crate out of the hole, up to the surface of the desert. They took a tool and were able to pry open the lid. They took out one of the lamps. My dad showed them how to set it up to collect solar rays to charge it, and they were soon busy setting up all the lamps in the crate, all forty-eight of them.

Meanwhile, the others who were still down in the hole were working on getting out another crate.

"*Shu fi?*" one man asked, and the writing on this crate I could understand.

"Computers!" I shouted, excited, at first, then

disappointed when I realized we would not be able to use them without electricity. "Oh, too bad we can't use them," I said, trying to not let my disappointment show. This was a field where I could be an expert, something I could teach the others so they would not think I was useless — but even if we had any electricity, which we didn't, how could we use computers in the desert?

"Why we cannot use them?" Jamal demanded. He gave me a stern look. "You think we not are smart like you?"

"No, I did not mean that at all," I said, shaking my head. "Computers need electricity. Do you guys have electricity?" Maybe they had it and I just didn't know.

My dad jumped into the hole and helped them unearth the crate. He seemed to be very excited about this discovery. They pulled the crate open, revealing boxes and boxes of what looked to be mini-computers, flat screens or something. I had never seen a computer as small as these boxes.

"We can use these computers!" my dad shouted. "These are solar powered!" He ripped open one box to reveal a tiny computer, just a screen, actually, and pulled it out of its protective covering.

"What these are for?" Nadir asked.

"These are some of the new computers the military had in storage," my dad said. "We have uncovered the storage area, so we should be finding quite a lot of useful tools in here. Let's keep digging, and we can charge these computers and use them later. I'm not sure how useful they are to us now, but we will be able to use them for something, I have no doubt."

The other men looked at him uncertainly, but they kept digging.

"Over there!" my dad shouted, near where Nadir was digging with a shovel. "I think that's a box of tools!"

The men dug for quite awhile until they were able to extract a very large crate from a deep hole. The men were getting very sweaty, and I realized the temperature was rising along with the sun.

When they were able to pry open the crate, they found some huge machine-things that could be used for digging, along with some smaller hand tools, including hammers, drills and tool kits. One item looked like a large shovel with wheels and levers and another item was like a big digging-bucket type of thing on wheels. These were tools I had never seen before, so I could not begin to name or even describe them, but I knew they could be used to make our task easier, or at least possible.

As soon as they pulled the items out of the crate, they decided to let the solar batteries charge the tools and get out of the sun. I waited for my dad to come out of the big hole so we could walk together to the tents.

When everyone was safely up and out of the hole, we all went to the three tents. One man said something that I did not understand, and my dad explained the plan to me.

"We three men with daughters will stay with you girls in that tent. The others will stay in those two tents. We will eat in the tents and then rest until tonight. As the sun goes down, we will eat again, then we will set up the lighting so we can work all night."

I followed the other two girls into our tent where blankets had been spread on the sand. The dads followed me.

"We sleep here," Lena said, pointing to one side of the tent, "fathers sleep over there."

We took our places on the blankets and Salwa served us the food they had been cooking: meat and bread with those potato-looking things I had prepared, which, by the way, were delicious, along with some small, stubby carrots. We drank water sparingly from our packs, then I stretched out to take a nap as Salwa collected the towels that had held our food. The day was warm, but inside the tent we were quite cool and comfortable. I heard the beginning of a conversation before I drifted into a deep sleep.

As I awakened, I had to remind myself where I was and what we were doing. Darkness was beginning to fall, the air was getting cooler, and I heard the sounds of snoring. I started to sit up but was pulled down by an arm across my shoulders. Before I could protest, warm breath whispered in my ear.

"I love you to be my wife and I marry you," he said, clearly and quietly.

I gasped and he clapped his hand over my mouth.

"You must accept and not tell," he insisted, right in my ear.

I struggled to get up, pushing hard against his arm. I did not know who he was or how he had gotten into our tent, but I knew I had to get away from him immediately.

"Where is the bathroom?" I asked loudly, and he quickly let me go.

I heard someone begin to stir, and my dad said, "Layla?"

"Yes, I wonder where I can go to the bathroom?" I crawled to the flap of the tent, to get away from the intruder.

"Go back behind the tent and dig a hole," my dad instructed. "Here is some tissue."

He must have had the tissue handy, because he put it directly into my hand. I scampered out of the tent, watching to see who would be coming out behind me, but no one followed me. I went behind the tent and dug a hole.

When I came back to the front of the tent, most of the people were busy, working on setting up the lighting. I could see a couple people already over by the excavation site, working with the big digging tools. They had several lanterns burning and that area was well-lit. My dad came out of the tent, and I had no reason to go back inside and possibly be trapped with the man who had whispered frightful things to me. I was not ready to get married! I had just found my dad, after being apart for nearly a decade, and I was enjoying being his daughter again. I was not in any position to suddenly become a man's wife, or even think about it yet. I was still a kid!

I looked for any sign of the person who had been whispering to me, but no guys were looking in my direction. Nobody was doing anything out of the ordinary. Who could it have been? Was it the father to one of the girls? Or was it one of the boys? I counted the men and all were out of the tents. I glanced over to our tent and I saw part of a blanket sticking out the side, underneath. I discovered how a boy could have gotten into the tent, just by lifting the edge and rolling under it.

Salwa and Lena were handing bundles of food to the men as they headed toward the work area. As Nadir and Jamal approached the girls, I noticed both girls smiling shyly at them then looking away from them, as the boys seemed to be flirting. The boys got their meals and walked away laughing. My dad and I were the last to claim our food from the girls.

"I could have helped you with that," I said apologetically.

"You new, you learn," Salwa said. "Eat and rejoy."

"Rejoy?" I asked.

"I not say that right?" She looked worried.

"She mean to say 'enjoy,'" Lena corrected.

"EN-joy," Salwa said, testing the word. "EN-joy."

"I will enjoy it. Thank you," I said, carrying my food to a group of small stones we had been using as chairs.

My dad joined me instead of going with the other men. He must have seen the puzzled look on my face. "I will go over there after I eat. I want to sit with you for a few minutes."

Those words were treasures to my ears. I had been wanting to sit with my dad, even for just a few minutes, for so many years, and now it was finally possible.

"Bless us, oh, Lord, for this food we are about to receive, and bless the hands that prepared it, in Jesus' mighty name, Amen," he prayed.

"Amen," I repeated, glad that I hadn't started eating yet. In the Time Before, we prayed every morning when we first got out of bed, every evening before we went to bed, and before every meal. After The Great Devastation, while I was living at the Complex, any acknowledgement of God was forbidden, so I had been able to pray only inside my head. I could not risk a prayer being heard by the listening devices which were abundant inside the Complex, or by the monitors which were hidden all over the place outside the Complex. We had almost no privacy, and any type of religion or spiritual life was not allowed. They wanted us to all think alike and act alike and not cause any problems by having feelings or loving anyone or thinking in any direction that may contradict the harmony of Complex life. I was so glad to be free of that complex life!

I redirected my thoughts to the present, my wonderful life with my dad. He was the best dad anyone could ever have, and he was sitting right here, next to me.

"What are you thinking about so intently?" my dad asked.

"Thinking about?" I said, snapping out of my drifting thoughts and smiling at him.

"You haven't taken one bite yet, and your eyes were so far away from here," he observed.

"I was just thinking about how thankful I am to be here with you, finally. I missed you so much. You have no idea how many times I wished for the impossible, to see you again and talk to you again, knowing in my mind it could never come true, but wishing it with all my heart. And now, here we are, together again!"

"'With God, all things are possible,'" he said, quoting a familiar Bible passage that I had forgotten.

"And I am SO thankful!" I said.

"Meeee toooo," he said. "You better eat, we have lots to do tonight."

I must have been daydreaming for quite some time, since he was finished with his food and I hadn't started mine yet. I ate my meal quickly, another delicious meal prepared by the two girls, and wondered what we were going to do next.

"Do you want me to help you?" I asked Lena and Salwa, who were sitting across from us and eating their meals, not nearly as rushed as I had been.

Lena shook her head. "We will rest now and begin to prepare our morning meal later. You rest too?"

"I want to help my dad," I said.

My dad began to stand up. "Come on, then, let's go." He gave me his hand, his strong, soft, warm and wonderful hand, and pulled me to my feet. I shook the crumbs from our towels and handed them to Salwa.

"Thank you, it was so good," I told the girls.

"You are welcome," they said together, in perfect English. They looked at each other and giggled. I hoped to soon be part of their little giggle group. I so loved being here, but I wanted to belong here, to have friends and things we could laugh about together.

My dad and I walked over to the big hole and looked at the progress. The men had pulled several more crates to the surface, revealing boxes of shovels, rakes, brooms and some kinds of cutters, among other things that I did not recognize. Each man now had a shovel, and Nadir's father, Nadir Senior, was driving the big digger.

"Wow, they have really made progress," I noted.

"Looks like we will have to move to another area," my dad said.

As I looked more closely, I understood why. They

were standing on top of a huge slab, probably one of the walls of the compound or the mall. Even with the new tools they had, they would not be able to break it into pieces. They would have to go around it.

One of the men came out of the hole and discussed something with my dad, who pointed toward the west. After the man scampered back into the hole, my dad explained what he had said.

"Jalal was asking which direction we should go next. I directed him that way, since I think we have all the tools we will ever need. I think we should begin to look for clothing now."

"Do you think there is anything else down there that we could use?" I asked.

"I really can't say, at this point. How many shovels do we need? Do we need dishes or appliances or televisions or furniture?"

"Maybe some furniture would be nice," I suggested.

"Perhaps at a later date. We can move much of the sand toward the east, since the wind always comes through here from the west, and make this an ongoing project, to dig up things to help improve our society."

"Improve our society? I think it's already so great. How can we improve it?"

"You know the nature of man, always wanting more, wanting better, wanting to make life easier." He sighed. "Besides the clothing, I honestly don't think we will find many things that can help us to improve our society, but I do not want to intrude on any ambitions these men — and boys — might have. They never had the chance to live the way we did, before the bombings, so they have some ideas."

"That makes sense," I agreed, rubbing my arms. The temperature was dropping and I was wearing short sleeves.

"Are you cold?" my dad asked, worried.

"Just a little chilly, but I can get a sweater out of my pack."

"I need to get down there and help with the digging and moving of our equipment to the new location, but maybe you want to check out one of the computers?" He must have seen the excitement in my eyes when he said that, and he smiled. "We charged up some of them during the day. They are in one of the tents. Ask the girls, and maybe you can show them how to use them, if you can figure it out."

"I can!" I almost shouted. Sure, the computers were old, but they were the newest type of technology — or were they the only type of technology? — around here.

"I'll see you in the morning, at breakfast time," he said, giving me a kiss on my forehead.

"Okay, I'll see you, Daddy." I felt like skipping back to the tents, but I discovered that it was not so easy to skip in the sand.

Lena and Salwa were just about to go inside our tent when they saw me hurrying towards them.

"What is the matter?" Lena asked.

"They did find clothes?" Salwa said.

"No, no, not yet," I said, short of breath. "I was wondering if we can look at the computers."

Both of them had the same expression, as their eyes went from bright to brighter in the glow of the lamp lights. I had not noticed when darkness had fallen, but it was here, now.

"You know how?" Salwa asked me.

"I am going to try to figure it out," I said.

She nodded her head as she understood the meaning of my sentence. Lena ducked into one of the tents and brought out a computer. Out of the box, it was tiny, just about ten by seven inches, and about a quarter inch thick. Lena handed it to me and the girls stared at me, waiting for me to do something amazing with it. I had an idea to get them more involved than just watching me.

"Are there more that are charged up, out of the box?" I asked Lena. "Bring out two more and we can each use one."

"We not know to read English," Salwa said.

"You can just do what I do," I said enthusiastically. "I'll teach you."

Lena dove back into the tent and quickly returned with two more of the mini computers as I examined the one in my hand. First, I would have to figure out how to open it. It was flat, blank on both sides, and had a small slit between the top and bottom. I tried sticking my fingernail between but nothing happened. It appeared to be sealed shut.

"We need to see how they open," I told the girls, as they were imitating what I was doing, turning, looking, trying to pry apart the two sides. "Let's go in the tent so we can sit down."

Lena and Salwa each grabbed a lamp and we took the computers into our tent. We got comfortable on our blankets and resumed our examinations of the computers. The thought occurred to me that we had so many computers, probably at least 60, so if we broke one or two, we would have more than enough for everyone to have have at least three to play with.

"It is lock," Salwa said. "How it unlock?"

I held the computer close to a lamp so I could look for any type of latch or button, but there was nothing on the top or bottom. I tried to remember something about these computers from when I was a little girl, but I was sure I had never seen one like this.

"Not useful," Lena said, tossing hers onto the blanket. "No good."

I had an idea as I was trying to think the way the military did when my dad worked for them. They made things to be easy to use and foolproof.

"Open," I said, clearly and distinctly, to the computer.

The top and bottom slowly began to split until they were at a right angle to each other, joined at one side. I set it on my lap so the screen was facing me and the keyboard was right in my lap. However, the keyboard had no letters or numbers on it.

"Open!" Salwa said loudly, and both hers and Lena's computers slowly opened. They put them in their laps, following my example, and looked to me for the next direction.

"Language?" my computer asked me, startling us so that we all jumped.

"English," I answered, and the keyboard instantly had lighted numbers, letters and symbols on it. I was so happy to see that the order of letters on the keyboard had not changed. This was the keyboard layout that I knew.

Their computers then asked for their language and they both answered them with "Arabic."

"Look!" Lena said proudly, turning her computer toward me. The keyboard was showing the Arabic alphabet and numbers. I looked closely at mine and saw that each key was actually a little monitor, changeable. The screen was blank.

"Setup complete," my computer stated. "Location services. Time zone. Weather. Calendar. Camera. Video. Conference. Telephone. Calculator. Database. Books. News. Messages. Address book. Settings. More."

"Messages?" I asked, as Lena's and Salwa's computers were speaking to them in Arabic. I presumed they were saying the same thing as mine, in their language.

"No messages," my computer answered.

"Maybe we can just speak to them," I said.

"How to change to English?" Lena asked me.

I shook my head as her computer asked her a question ending with the word '*Ingleezi.*'

Lena giggled. "I tell computer change to English," she said excitedly.

"Change to English?" her computer asked.

"Change to English!" she said. She turned her keyboard to me and I saw that the letters and numbers had changed to the English language.

"Location services?" I asked my computer, wondering what exactly what it had meant when it listed the applications.

"Searching... searching," the computerized voice

said. "Location classified."

"How can this work?" I asked. "No computers or servers exist to give it information."

"Repeat question," my computer told me.

"How does this computer work?" I asked.

"Solar power. Lo-duck technology. Satellite services. Voice or device activated. Did I answer your question?"

"Yes," I said, putting it together in my head. The military must have had these programmed to receive information from a satellite, so even though all the computer networks were destroyed, these still worked.

"Telephone," I said, taking a chance. Would I really be able to call someone?

"Out of range," the computer said. I tried to remember what Kenrick, my genius friend, had said about this valley. Some kind of magnetic block or something prevented signals from getting to this area. I didn't understand how that worked with the satellite services, but maybe we could get a different response once we were back home, at the hut village.

I got a little bit excited when I thought of the small community of huts as being my home. A few huts filled with love were more of a home to me than the high-tech, tightly controlled Complex life ever had been.

Lena and Salwa were talking and typing on their computers, having figured out how to do something with them.

"We send message!" Salwa said triumphantly.

"Who can you send a message to?" I asked. I didn't know of anyone else in the world who had a computer like this one, and I doubted they could send a message back to someone at the Complex — unless, maybe, Kenrick. Yes, that was possible.

"To Lena!" Salwa said happily. I smiled as I watched them send messages back and forth to each other, thinking that soon I would be able to also send them a message.

I decided to try something. I composed a message, searched for users on the network and found just two, written in Arabic letters. I typed a short message, "Hi, this is Layla. How are you?" then quietly told my computer to translate message to Arabic and send to the two users.

Both girls stopped what they were doing and looked at me in astonishment.

"You know to write Arabic?" Salwa asked, her eyes wide.

"No, I wrote in English and told it to translate to Arabic."

"Yes, yes!" Lena said. She quickly typed a message and sent it to me. It was written in Arabic, so I asked the computer to translate to English.

"Read aloud?" the computer asked me.

"No," I instructed. Underneath the Arabic sentence it printed, "I am fine, thank you."

We continued experimenting with the little computers and discovered how to use the calendar, how to read books on screen or have them read aloud to us, and how to use the camera. The greatest discovery was the videoconference application that allowed us to see and talk to each other through the computers. Granted, it was not so spectacular to be able to have a videoconference with two people who were sitting right across from me, but this could be very useful when we went on a hunting and gathering adventure. We could even use it right now, while we were in the tent and the guys were digging, just a short distance away from us, but out of sight.

After spending two or three hours playing with our new computers, my eyes were getting very tired. I felt some eye strain looking at the bright screen in our dark tent. I looked away from the screen to give my eyes a rest and suddenly I felt like I could very easily take a nap. I glanced over at my blanket and Salwa must have been watching me.

"You feel tired," she stated.

"Yes, I think I will rest for a while," I said, feeling my whole body wanting to relax.

"Please excuse me," Salwa said, "I may braid your hair?" she said apologetically.

I nearly panicked. I had not thought about the condition of my hair since the day I arrived at my dad's hut! I had not seen myself in a mirror. I knew my curls must look like a tangled mess. When Lena and Salwa had their hoods down, their long and beautiful dark braids hung down their backs. I realized they probably braided each other's hair, since it seemed not possible for a girl to be able to braid her own hair and have it look that nice. Back at the Complex, we had Hair Managers who took care of the needs of our hair, from selecting a style to cutting it, washing it and styling it as often as we needed. They kept my hair at a medium length and I usually went to them three or four times a week.

"I think it's too short to braid," I said, desperately wanting my hair to look as nice as theirs did.

"I can," Salwa said kindly. "I show you."

I could not resist her offer to help me look better by taking care of my questionable hair. She pulled a brush out of her pack and moved over to sit behind me. She was so gentle with my hair, I just relaxed while she brushed, separated and pulled my hair into shape.

"Lena," Salwa said, after only a few minutes, "look at her hair."

"It is beautiful," Lena said, her eyes glowing with approval.

"I want to see it," I said, already knowing how much better it must have looked than it had just a few minutes ago.

"I have, how you say it, *mur-uh,*" Lena said, digging through her pack.

"Mirror," I said, as she handed one to me.

"Almost it is the same," Salwa said.

I looked at my reflection with a new respect for Salwa, as well as for myself. With my hair pulled back from my face and every strand in place, I looked more mature, my face more refined. "No, it is NOT the same, it is so much better this way! Thank you, Salwa!" These girls had so many talents. I had so much to learn.

"No, I mean to say, words almost the same with the sound," Salwa explained, "mirror, *mur-uh.*"

"Yes, they do have similar sounds," I agreed, turning the mirror to see the sides of my head, the top of my head. My hair looked great, but I would have to wash it very soon. "Where do you wash your hair?"

We were interrupted by shouting from the men. I heard the pounding of feet on the sand and all at once,

Nadir and Jamal were leaning into our tent, breathing hard and fast.

"We found something!" Nadir said. At the same time, Jamal said something in Arabic, and I assumed he was relating the same message to the other girls.

"*Ma-huwa*?" Lena asked.

"What is it?" I said.

We scrambled to follow the boys back to where the men were digging, asking questions while we were running. We couldn't get any answers from them, but I was sure they had found something quite amazing. My mind raced as I considered the possibilities. Did they find the clothing? Sporting goods? Solar electrical generators? Solar-powered refrigerators? More food? Bigger and better computers? Communication devices? Transportation?

I never would have imagined what we saw once we arrived at the hole, which was now much deeper and wider than it had been just a few hours ago: all the men and the other two boys were gone!

"*Ween hamma*?" Lena demanded, just as I said, "Where is everyone? Where is my dad?"

"Come with us, *yalla*," Nadir said, sliding down into the hole on one side that was less steep than the other.

Jamal began to follow Nadir, then turned to help us slip down into the hole. He helped Lena first, then Salwa, and they ran across the bottom surface of the hole behind Nadir. As Jamal grabbed my arm, he intentionally pulled me close to him, put his arm around me, and guided me down the side, to the bottom. He kept his arm around me, even after we arrived, and held my body close to his as we made our way, somewhat more slowly, across the hole. He whispered something in my ear that made me feel tingly, even though I could not understand what he was saying. Then he suddenly stopped, still holding me, stopping me with him, and he turned to me and kissed me on the lips!

I was shocked! I had never been kissed before! I pulled my face away from his, afraid of him, afraid of his intentions. I merely wanted to find my dad and see whatever this great discovery had been. I was not prepared for romance or anything like it!

I quickly snatched myself out of his arms and ran to catch the others, to see what they were seeing as they stopped and stared down at something. My sudden movements must have startled Jamal, since he was no longer right with me.

"What is it?" I yelled to the others, out of breath, for more than one reason. My heart was pounding and I felt slightly terrified of Jamal. I knew I would never be able to be alone with him; he was too forward, too pushy for me.

I was really panting as I caught up to where Nadir, Salwa and Lena were standing. I gasped when I looked down into a deeper part of the hole and finally got a look at what they could see.

CHAPTER 5

We were looking at a door, an open door. As my eyes adjusted to the darker darkness, with just a sliver of light somewhere very deep, I was able to make out a ladder going down. It was impossible to see how long the ladder was or where it went.

"Are they inside there?" I asked.

"Yes, they went to explore," Nadir said.

"Let us go inside!" Lena said, stepping towards the ladder.

"Some must stay out," Jamal said, as he joined the little group.

I was not about to be the only one left outside with Jamal.

"I need to go inside and find my dad," I insisted, pushing past Lena.

"Yes," Nadir agreed. "You go down, inside, with your dad, and we stay. Your dad is guide."

I wasn't sure what he meant by that, but I did not want to stay and ask questions. I began to step on the rungs of the ladder.

"Why not we all go?" Salwa asked, sounding a little like she might be pouting.

"If something happen, some need to stay out," Jamal explained.

"I have an idea!" I shouted, stopping after just a few steps. "We can use the computers to communicate!"

"Computers?" Nadir asked, looking from me to Salwa to Lena.

"Yes!" Lena agreed. "Layla, you wait, I go get the computers. You take one for communicate." She took off running toward the tent.

"Computers?" Nadir asked again.

"We took three of the computers that were charged up and we set them up and we were testing them and trying to do different things with them," I said quickly. I was so excited about what was happening, I could not remain calm.

Jamal stepped close to me and reached his hand toward my head. I flinched, afraid of what he was going to do, but he just touched my hair.

"You now have little braid," he said, smiling.

"Yes, Salwa made it for me," I said, increasing the distance between us.

"You do this?" Jamal asked her.

Salwa smiled shyly at him. "Yes. She nice hair."

"Yes, she have nice hair," Jamal said, trying to correct her English.

"Yes, she has nice hair," Nadir corrected them both.

"She did a good job," I said, in an attempt to direct their attention away from me and my hair.

"You go in, down?" Salwa asked Nadir and Jamal as she looked into the opening in the ground.

"No, we go back to get you," Jamal said.

"What are they doing down there?" I asked, also trying to get a look into the darkness. I was not able to hear anything that was happening inside the tunnel or cave or whatever it was, but I was certainly curious.

"They explore down there," Nadir said.

Lena suddenly rushed over to us carrying a backpack with her. I hadn't even seen her slide down into the hole, she was just there with us.

"This one yours," she said, pulling one of the computers from the pack and handing it to me.

I took it from her, then wondered how I was going to go down the ladder with a computer in my hands.

"I carry computer for you," Jamal suggested, as Nadir took the computer from me.

"You, Layla, go down first, I follow you with computer," Nadir instructed. "Lena, Salwa, stay with Jamal."

Jamal said something in Arabic and I had a feeling it was not a phrase of kindness, but I stepped onto the ladder and began climbing into the hole.

"You not afraid?" Salwa asked, as my head became level with the ground.

"No, I am not afraid," I said. I wondered why she had asked that, and a slight feeling of fear came over me, but I kept moving down into the hole. I was trying to see where the ladder ended, and I heard Nadir above me, following me. I kept feeling for the next rung with my foot, and there kept being another step, another step, another step. Soon I was in complete darkness, unable to see a thing, and one foot came in contact with what felt to be a cement floor.

"How you doing?" Nadir asked.

"I think I am at the bottom," I said, stepping away from the ladder so he would not step on my head. I was standing under the ground, in the dark. I had no idea if I was in a large room or a small tunnel, but I could not see a thing.

"I am on bottom, too," Nadir said. "Here is computer. You can use it for light?"

Why hadn't I thought of that idea? I reached out until our hands met, which made me feel just a bit tingly, and I took the computer from him.

"Open," I said, and the computer opened and the screen became bright. I turned it around and held it out in front of me. As my eyes adjusted to the dim amount of light, I could see that we were in a small room that had several doorways which led to hallways or passageways going in different directions. I saw something on the wall near me, a paper or a poster, and I turned the computer to illuminate it.

"What it is?" Nadir asked.

"What is it?" I automatically corrected him. I was immediately sorry I had said that, but he didn't seem to mind.

"You can read it?"

"Yes, it says this was built by the military and inside is a map," I said. I unfolded the paper and another paper fell from inside it, to the floor. Nadir picked it up and opened it.

"This is a map," he confirmed.

"Wow, this place is enormous!" I said. The map showed rooms and corridors and storage closets that extended at least the entire size of the Military Quadrant. Upon closer inspection, I read the description that it had been built as a shelter in case of a disaster. I wondered if my parents had known about this. Surely everyone who lived in the Four Quadrants must have been informed of this place; but why had my dad not known about it?

Why had we evacuated instead of just coming down

here at the start of the war? What if some people had been down here? We might be able to find them now! According to this map, there were enough supplies stored to sustain human life for a hundred years... but for how many people? Perhaps only the leaders knew about this place. Perhaps only the most important people in the Four Quadrants had access to the shelter. However, how important could they be now, after being hidden for all these years? No wonder my dad was guiding the group. He probably knew where the other people were hiding, or at least he would be able to figure out the most likely place they would be.

I examined the map to see if I could get an idea of which way they had gone. Just when I was about to give up, when it seemed there were too many possibilities to narrow it down to one way, I had an idea.

"Computer," I said, "Show me the map."

"Clarification needed," the computer replied. "Map of what?"

"You talk to computer and computer talk back?" Nadir asked, astonished.

"Show me the map of where we are, underground in the Military Quadrant of the Four Quadrants."

"Showing the map," the computer said.

We looked at the screen and saw a duplicate of the paper map Nadir was holding, only on the screen it was three-dimensional.

"Holy cow!" Nadir exclaimed.

I smiled when he said that. I would need to help him select more modern expressions, but that was not my concern at this moment.

"Computer, where are we on this map?"

"You are here." A glowing green spot appeared at one corner of the map.

Nadir leaned in closer to see.

"Computer, are other people in this map?"

"People are here, here and here." Little orange clusters appeared in three locations on the computerized map.

"These three must be Jamal and Salwa and Lena," I said, pointing to three small dots near our location. "The others must have split up, that is why there are two groups over here and here."

"Computer, show me the way to this large group of people," I said, touching the screen where one of the orange clusters was.

"Route one," the computer said, drawing a blue line which took a direct path from us to them. "Route two," it said, drawing a second, less direct path in lighter blue.

"That is amazing," I said.

"Not amazing. Direct route and indirect route," the computer stated.

"Let's go," I said, moving toward the doorway following the most direct route.

Nadir was right behind me. I looked at the screen and I was able to see the green spot, us, moving along the blue line.

I had another idea. "Computer, brighten the screen."

This time, the computer didn't talk back to me, but the brightness of the screen became much more intense. I turned it so the screen faced in the direction we were going, to use it as a flashlight.

"You are very smart with computer," Nadir remarked.

"This is a very smart computer," I said.

"Thank you for the compliment," the computer said.

Nadir and I both laughed. I remembered Lena and Salwa and I stopped. Nadir bumped into me.

"I am so very sorry," he said, taking a step away from me.

"Oh, no, it was my fault," I said. "I just remembered why we brought the computer in the first place."

"Computer is working very well," Nadir said.

"Computer, start videoconference with Lena," I instructed.

"Close map?"

"No, open small videoconference window. Keep map open."

"Videoconference with Lena started."

I turned the screen to face me and I could see Lena, Salwa and Jamal looking into the camera on Lena's computer.

"We found a map!" I said. "We are going to where the men are."

"A map?" Lena asked.

Nadir began to speak rapidly in Arabic to them. They asked him a couple of questions and he answered them.

"Excuse my language," he said to me apologetically. "I want to explain very quickly what happens so they understand. We do not know English words for all we are doing."

"Oh, sure, that's fine," I said. "Let's keep the window open so they can see where we are going," I suggested. "We can keep talking while we are walking."

I turned the computer around so it was facing in front of us, to light our path.

"Too dark, cannot see anything," Lena said.

"Keep looking," Nadir said. "Our fathers are ahead of us."

"We do not see them," she said.

"We don't see them either," I said, "but we are looking. The computer is directing us to where they are."

"You know computer very well," Jamal said.

"I am learning how to use this one, and it is a very smart computer," I said. I felt better about him when we were not close to each other.

"I love to use computer!" Salwa said.

"It is very handy right now," I said.

"What is this, 'handy' you say?" Lena asked.

"I mean, it is very useful," I said, wondering if the computer had a translator for English idioms, then I was ashamed of myself for thinking that. We had plenty of time to spend together, and I could teach them. They did not need to rely on a computer to translate while I was here with them.

"It is very handy," Jamal said, trying out the expression.

We kept walking down the corridor with the computer giving us verbal prompts when to turn. We must have passed twenty doors to the left and right, and I was eager to look at the map later to see what was in all these rooms, but now, we just needed to find the men.

The screen suddenly became dim and I stopped, startled, unable to see the path ahead of us. Nadir was following so closely behind me that he again bumped into me.

"I am so sorry," he whispered in my ear, as he was standing, leaning over me. He was a lot taller than I was. He put his hands on my shoulders and I felt myself become tense. I did not want a repeat of Jamal's kiss forced upon me.

Nadir just held my shoulders gently and I could feel goose bumps going down my arms.

"It — it — it is okay," I whispered to him, not wanting the others to hear our conversation. Actually, I felt better than okay, but now was not the time to think about or even feel my attraction to this handsome young man.

"Computer?" I said. Immediately, the screen became brighter and we were able to see our way again.

"Out of power-saving mode," the computer stated.

We began to walk, and I pretended to not notice — or at least I didn't say anything about — the fact that Nadir was still holding onto my shoulders. I told myself he was just doing it for safety reasons, so he would not crash into me again. I pushed aside the other thoughts about him that wanted to pop into my mind and I concentrated on finding my dad.

"I hear them," Nadir said, as we rounded another corner.

"I do, too," I said, but we still could not see any light ahead of us. We kept walking, but a little more slowly.

"Turn right," the computer instructed.

I looked to the right as Nadir reached over and opened a door. Light flooded into the hallway where we were. We walked into what I would have thought was a party in progress, if I hadn't known why these men were here in the first place.

They were so busy, they did not notice us at first. Some men had on military work uniforms, some had on casual clothing, while others were wrapped in towels. I could smell soap, shampoo, freshness, and I knew they had been taking showers. Men were drinking out of glasses and eating food from plates.

My dad saw me, and his face lit up. "Layla!" he said, and a few of the men turned toward us. I became aware that Nadir's hands were no longer touching me, and I was glad about that.

"Did you know about this place?" I asked my dad.

"I had heard of it, but I did not know where it was, or if it had been completed," he explained. "When we lived here, in the Four Quadrants, we were informed that a shelter would be built underground, in case of emergencies. As you can see, it is functionally complete, but they were not finished with it. They did stock it with food and clothing and —"

"And it has running water!" I exclaimed. I was thrilled at the prospect of being able to take a shower.

"So, you were able to figure out the computer?" he asked.

"Oh, yes!" I had temporarily forgotten about our companions who were waiting so patiently outside for us. I turned the computer to face me, and I saw Lena, Salwa and Jamal looking intently into the camera.

"We found them!" I said.

Several of the men crowded around us, looking at the computer.

"We see light and all the group," Lena said.

"*Shu hatha*?" Lena's dad asked me.

I turned the computer so he could see his daughter on the screen. "We have on the videoconference, there's Lena and Salwa and Jamal, they are waiting outside, and also, it has a map. That is how we found you."

The men, most of them now pressing in close to see the computer, looked quite impressed and amazed. I felt a little bit proud that I had been able to do something they probably didn't know how to do, even though I wasn't a Comgen, a computer genius.

Lena said something in Arabic to her father, and he answered her. I handed the computer to him and I turned to my dad.

"We should stay down here, instead of in the tents," I suggested.

"Why don't you pick out some other clothes, and you can take a shower?" my dad said to me. That was my cue to take care of myself and not to try to make any decisions for the entire group, and I nodded.

"Nadir," his dad said, and Nadir went over to talk to him.

"Go into this room," my dad said, pointing to an open door. It was then that I realized the rooms were being lit by electrical lighting and the lanterns were sitting on a table near the door. "Find some clothes that are your size, then you can go in that shower room, over there, where you will have some privacy. The men are using the other shower room, back over there."

I walked into a storage room where stacks of clothing were piled on shelves, each outfit individually vacuum-sealed in plastic. I found some that seemed to be my size and I looked through the selection. Many of them were military outfits, but underneath were some casual clothes and some civilian clothes. I opened a one of the packages and discovered that the outfit was way too large for me. I moved to a stack that was labeled as a smaller size and opened another of the packages. Now I had the size right, but once I got it out of the plastic, I could see that the color was unpleasant. I did not want to wear olive green and black, if I had a choice. I did have a choice, so I opened a package that was labeled 'blue.' This color was more to my liking, so I headed toward the shower room with my change of clothing.

As I stepped inside, I noticed a shelf with about a hundred towels, so I grabbed a large one and a small one and prepared for a heavenly experience — a shower. I also found a box of new combs, so I took out a red one to use. I closed the door behind me and turned on the water. I took my hair out of the braid as I waited for the water to get warm.

CHAPTER 6

When I was all fresh and clean — how long had I been in there, anyway? — with wet and combed hair and wearing a new outfit, I was just about to open the door when it was pulled open from the other direction.

"Oh, you scared me!" I said, as Lena and Salwa were stepping into the shower room. "Did you find some clothes?"

They both nodded happily, and I could see they were as eager as I had been to take a shower.

"There are the towels," I said, pointing to the shelves.

"Towels," Salwa repeated, as they grabbed towels.

As I was leaving the room, I heard her call to me, "I braid your hair again?"

"Yes, please, when you get finished!" I said. "Take your time, no hurry!"

I rejoined my dad and the others feeling like a new person, but I needed one more thing.

"Daddy," I said, "do you know if they have any toothbrushes here?"

"Oh, yes, my darling daughter," he said. He went to a cupboard and opened it, revealing about a thousand toothbrushes individually sealed in plastic and shelves of bottles of toothpaste. He took one of each and handed them to me.

"Thank you," I said. "I'll be right back!" I dashed back to the shower room and went to the sink to brush my teeth. Now, with clean teeth and fresh breath, I felt better than ever. I rejoined the group, minus Lena and Salwa, who were still in the shower room.

The men were all huddled in a group, looking at something. My dad saw me come into the room and he quickly came over to me.

"The computer," he said excitedly, "we think there are others here, in this shelter!"

"What?" I asked, trying to push my way into the huddle.

"Layla!" Nadir said, and the group parted to let me inside. "The map, remember? How we find this room?"

"Yes," I said, and then I did remember: another cluster of people on the map, which we had assumed was part of our group. I quickly counted the people in the room, which actually was unnecessary, but I had to be sure everyone in our group was in this room. I looked at the screen and I could see another cluster of people — maybe five people? — in another part of the shelter.

"Who are they?" I asked my dad.

Everyone in the room looked at him for the answer.

He shook his head and shrugged his shoulders. "I have no idea."

"Let's go find them!" I said excitedly.

"*La-a,*" one of the men said, and I knew that meant 'no.' He said a bunch of things rapidly in Arabic, and I could not understand even one word.

Nadir stepped over near me and explained, "We do not know if they are safe. They may be enemies. We must be careful."

"How can they be our enemies?" I asked. "We have so few people left on earth, we have to live together and to work together."

Lena and Salwa came into the room, all fresh and clean, drying their hair with towels. Lena had selected a deep red outfit and Salwa was wearing a pretty, dark green outfit.

"I will go," my dad volunteered. "I might know them."

"And I'll go with you!" I said. "They won't do anything to you if I am with you."

The men looked at my dad and at me, considering this possibility.

"You all wait here," my dad said, "or go outside, if you feel safer out there, and I will go, Layla and I will go, and find out who they are. Maybe they have been down here all these years and they don't know what is going on outside."

"Maybe they think they are the only ones left in the world," I added. After all, I had just discovered my dad and his tribe, and they had thought they were the only ones left in the world.

"I go with you," Nadir said. "You might need translator."

His dad looked at him intently. He slowly nodded his head. "You go," he finally said.

"You take computer with you," Lena said.

Her dad, who had been holding my computer (it wasn't really mine, but it was the one I had been using), handed it to me. My dad grabbed a lantern and handed it to Nadir, then picked up a flashlight and another lantern. That much light would allow us to be able to see a lot better than the light of the computer screen.

"We prepare food. We eat when you return," Jamal

said, nodding to Lena and Salwa, who nodded along with him.

"Let us go now," my dad said, leading the way.

"Take careful," Lena's dad said.

"*Baba*, you say 'be careful,' not 'take careful,'" Lena said with a little laugh.

"We will be careful," I assured them, as I followed my dad out the door, into the hallway.

Nadir stepped behind me and closed the door.

"Computer," I said, "show the route to the other people."

"Route one, direct route," the computer said, adding a line in blue from us to where it said the other people were. "Route two, indirect route." A light blue line appeared from us to them following a more roundabout way to get to them.

"I think we should take the direct route," I said.

"Let me take a look at that," my dad said, pausing to see the screen. "Yes, that's a good idea. They are actually quite a long ways from us. We better get moving."

We walked at a rather rapid pace, stopping every once in awhile so my dad could check the map to be sure we were on the right track. We had been walking for about ten minutes when my dad checked to see how close we were. He was surprised by what he saw.

"They are moving!" he said. "Now we need to turn right, or we will miss them."

I looked at the screen and sure enough, the little orange dots were on the move. The computer reconfigured the trail so we could easily intersect with them.

We began trotting, anxious to catch up with them, and as we rounded a corner, we heard shouting.

"Halt! In the name of the law!" a man's voice shouted at us. Bright lights shone in our faces and we could not see anything but the lights. I held up my arm to protect my eyes.

"We come in peace," my dad said, to my relief. He always was a quick thinker.

"Who are you?" the same voice asked.

"I was about to ask you that very question," my dad said.

"You are not authorized to be here," the man said. "We have thousands of troops surrounding you, and you will be put under arrest. Surrender your weapons."

"Weapons?" my dad said. "We don't have any weapons. Look, I have two children with me, well, teenagers, anyway. We have no weapons."

"What is that you have, that device?" he shouted, stepping closer to us.

"This?" I asked, holding it out to him. "This is a computer."

"You have a computer?" he asked angrily.

"Beezeeneck?" my dad said, closing the distance between him and the man. "Is that you, Beezeeneck?"

Nadir and I must have been frozen in our tracks. We did not move, but if my dad knew this man, that seemed like a good sign.

"How do you know my name?" the man insisted. "Are you scanning me with that computer?"

My dad laughed. "Beezeeneck! It IS you!" He closed

the gap between them so the man could get a good look at him. "Don't you remember me?"

"Obiad?" the man asked. "Obiad, is it you? But how can it be? You were killed in the air raid! Nobody survived the attack!"

"I survived," my dad said. "The Bible literally saved my life. I was in the warehouse preparing the Bibles for distribution and the building collapsed, but the Bibles protected me. They made a kind of shelter around me. When I was finally able to get out of the rubbish that had been the warehouse, I was the only one left."

"What are you talking about? There were no survivors except the few of us who were working down here when the air raid came. We saw the reports on the satellite feed. No one could survive the toxicity outside of this underground shelter. We were the only ones left. Where have you really been hiding?"

"It must have not been toxic," my dad said, "because I was out there all this time and it didn't kill me, and there are others still alive. We just found this place today, and we discovered we were not the only ones here, so we came to find you, and here we are."

"You say there are others?" Beezeeneck asked suspiciously, looking around to find them. "How many others?"

"We have twenty-four in our group," my dad said, then he corrected himself. "Make that twenty-five, now that my daughter is here."

"This is little Layla?" he asked in astonishment, examining me closely. "This is little Layla? Come, come into our lounge and have a seat."

We followed him into a nicely decorated room and

sat in some comfortable chairs. I sat by my dad and Nadir sat beside me.

"Yes, I am his daughter, Layla," I confessed. I still had no idea who this man was.

"What do you mean, now that she is here? Where was she before?" he asked, taking a seat on a chair across from us

"Layla?" my dad said, turning the floor over to me.

"I came with some friends from a part of what used to be the United States. We came to explore the area where the war had started, where the beginning of The Great Devastation had been, and I found a cemetery and that led me to find my dad. We came from a place called The Complex, where we lived and worked, and I think about six hundred people live there. Plus there are the Outsiders, and I have no idea how many of them there are. They live in clusters around the State. But, you must understand, the State is so much smaller than when it was a country, in the Time Before. There were earthquakes and floods, and entire chunks of the country were swallowed up by the ocean. I don't know, maybe a couple thousand people still live in the State? We had no idea there were any people on this side of the world until we came here and I found my dad."

"How many people are living here?" my dad asked, looking around the room. No one else was in the room with us.

"We have only five people left," Beezeeneck said sadly. "Nineteen were working down here when the air raid came, but we have lost fourteen."

"They died?" I asked. It did not seem likely to me that fourteen people had just gotten lost somewhere in this large compound.

"Four people left, they went outside the shelter, about a year after the air raid. They never came back. We never heard from them again, so we assumed they had died from the toxicity. Three years later, four more people left, and this time they took communicators with them, so they could stay in contact with us. They kept in contact for a couple of days as they started on a journey south, then we lost the signal, so we assumed they had also died.

"We had eleven people still living here. We planned to wait two more years before sending any more out, but one man got cabin fever and he took off in the middle of the night. We never heard from him again. After two years, four more decided to take the risk, and they stayed in contact with us for almost a week. They thought they had found something significant, but we lost their signal and we never heard from them again.

"The last person we lost was my wife. She died in childbirth about a year ago, and we were unable to save the baby. It was a boy." Beezeeneck stopped talking and swallowed hard. He seemed to be a little bit choked up.

"Oh, Beezeeneck, I am so sorry," my dad said.

"I'm sorry," I said also.

"The deaths were not your fault," Nadir whispered in my ear. "Why you are sorry?"

"I will explain later," I whispered to him, trying to not be rude.

"So, we are down to five," Beezeeneck said with a sigh. "Obiad, you knew just about everyone here, didn't you?"

"I did," my dad said, nodding. "I knew every person

in the Four Quadrants by name."

"I will make a list for you," Beezeeneck said, then he opened his eyes wide, as if he just remembered something. "That's right! The last expedition! Weren't you related to Steele? Pierce Steele?"

"Uncle Pierce?" I asked.

"He was my brother-in-law," my dad said, still nodding.

"Steele led the last expedition! The last group that left from here, Steele was the leader!" Beezeeneck was getting very excited, bobbing up and down in his chair.

"He survived the bombings?" my dad asked. "But how can that be possible?" Now he was shaking his head.

"As I recall, he was injured and another fellow, Harvey Wickersham, carried him down here just as the air raid began. It was all some kind of strange coincidence, but his injury saved both of their lives. Wickersham hadn't even planned to come down here that day, that fateful day when all of our lives were forever changed."

"Why did Wickersham bring Pierce down here?" my dad asked.

I was wondering the same thing, because Uncle Pierce was scheduled meet us on the plane my mom and my Aunt Moon and I were on, the only plane that was able to take off before the bombings started.

"I can't recall the details, I just remember he was carrying Steele and the doors were about to be automatically sealed. They just made it in at the last second, just as the doors were closing."

"So, Uncle Pierce is still alive?" I asked.

"He was when he walked out of here, a few years ago," Beezeeneck said, "but I can only assume he died out there, because we have not heard a thing from anyone who has left. We have had no more communication from them. Nobody has come back. We don't know what happened to them. Even if they didn't die from the toxicity, how could they survive out there?"

"The bombings were not toxic," my dad said. "I was out there for nine years and I didn't get sick, not even a little. You can see that I am still alive."

Beezeeneck examined my dad, as if to check whether he was telling the truth.

"So… how did you communicate with the ones who left here?" I asked. Even though I was just seventeen, I thought I might have had some knowledge about the situation that the men did not have.

"We used portable communication devices," Beezeeneck said. "Do you remember those, Obiad? We were just starting to use them to communicate, instead of the personal phones."

"I remember hearing about them," my dad said, nodding slowly, "but I hadn't received mine. I hadn't even seen one yet."

"We have lots of them down here," Beezeeneck said, getting out of his chair. "I can show you how they work. We had plenty of time to learn how to use them, once we were sealed inside of this place. Once we stopped getting the news reports, we didn't have much else to do besides explore, exercise and play with the PCDs, or port-coms."

"So, you were able to communicate with each other

while you were down here?" I asked.

"Yes, and we still do," Beezeeneck said, thumping his forehead with the palm of his hand. "I need to let the others know you are here! We picked up a signal from your computer, must have been the one you are holding, and we were trying to figure out if we had a computer malfunction or if we actually were picking up a signal. I'll call them to come over here and stop searching for a problem."

"We have more people here," Nadir said.

"Here?" Beezeeneck asked, stopping and looking around the room.

"In another part of this compound," my dad explained. "They waited while we came and looked for you."

"And you knew we were here because...?" Beezeeneck asked. He pulled a very small device from his pocket. It looked like a short, stubby pen.

"We saw you in the computer," I said. "Well, not you specifically, but we could see there were people here when we called up the map."

"Hold on a minute," Beezeeneck said, holding up one finger to suspend our conversation.

"Beezeeneck here. Wickersham, Conrad-Bean, Salmoony, Anita," he said into his port-com. "You can come on to the D-3 lounge."

"Conrad-Bean here. We have not, repeat, have NOT discovered the source of the disturbance," a high-pitched voice said through the PCD, loud enough for us to hear.

"Salmoony here. Neither have we, but we can

detect interference from the main frame," a deep voice reported.

"Beezeeneck here. We have visitors in the D-3 lounge. Return from your mission."

"Returning," Conrad-Bean said.

"We are returning," Salmoony said.

Beezeeneck put his port-com into his pocket and brought a chair over by me. He sat close enough to see the computer and he examined it closely. "Where did you get that?"

"We found a crate full of them outside," my dad said, "near the entrance on the west side."

"The entrance on the west side?" Beezeeneck asked. "But that entrance has been blocked since the air raid."

"We dug it up," my dad said. "We had a team digging, we were all digging—"

"We were actually looking for clothing for all of us, but we uncovered the entrance and we came in to see what it was," I interrupted.

My dad did not look pleased by my interruption, so I kept my mouth shut for awhile, even though I felt like I had some important information to share with all of them, information about their communication problems.

"Can I see it?" Beezeeneck asked, motioning for the computer.

I closed the videoconference window and handed him the computer, now showing only the map. For some reason, I did not want him to see Lena and the others, and I did not want them to see him yet.

"How many of these do you have?" he asked,

moving his hand over the screen, calling up programs that I had not discovered.

"Oh, probably at least sixty," my dad said.

"How many of you are here?" Beezeeneck demanded. He looked shocked.

"Only nineteen of us are here, inside the compound," my dad said, "but we have a few more back at our camp."

"Your camp? Where is your camp?"

"It is southeast of here, a few miles away," my dad said.

"And you have 60 computers?" Beezeeneck asked.

"We just found them — was it yesterday?" my dad asked, looking at Nadir and me.

We nodded. It seemed like a very long time ago, but it must have been yesterday.

"We have only opened a few of the boxes," my dad said.

"These were the latest model, nine years ago," Beezeeneck said, opening a program and reading something. "They were classified property, and now they are in the hands of civilians." He seemed disappointed.

"We have enough to go around," I said, wanting him to give mine back to me. By this time, I was attached to this particular computer, but he was not paying any attention to me. "Everyone can have his own computer." I tried to not sound like I was pouting, because I was not.

"So, on this map, here, you found us," Beezeeneck said, back to the screen with the map again. "I see, I see.

And it looks like, according to this map, the rest of my crew are just about to arrive."

My ears told me that before he said it, because I could hear voices in the hallway.

We all turned to look at the door as it opened. Four people came in, three men and one woman, talking and laughing, and they stopped and stared at us. My dad stood, so Nadir and I also stood. Beezeeneck was still looking at the computer screen and didn't pay much attention to his crew, as he had called them. I assumed that he was the one in charge.

My dad walked over to them, and I realized he probably knew all of them. One guy kind of looked familiar to me, and I may have seen the lady near our house in the Residential Quadrant, but now she was so thin. Yes, I was sure I had seen her before. My dad reached out to shake hands.

"Wickersham," he said, grabbing the hand of the first man.

"Maloof?" Wickersham answered, with a look of unbelief on his face. He was short and balding with a very friendly-looking face. "You are alive," he said, stating the obvious. I thought he was going to give my dad a hug, but he just stood there, staring at him.

"Yes," my dad said, letting go of his hand and moving to the next man. He was much taller than the rest, and he had rich, shiny black hair. "Salmoony."

"Mr. Maloof," Salmoony said. "I remember you, you were the chaplain."

"Yes, I was," my dad said. He held his hand for another few seconds, then turned to the next man and reached for his hand.

"Jason Conrad-Bean," my dad said. "You were stationed in the house next to ours, but you and your young bride never had a chance to live there. We were going to be neighbors."

"You remember that?" Jason said, his eyes clouding. "I have been trying to forget about that. I have no good memories of that house." He seemed like he was about to start crying.

"Of course," my dad said, putting his left hand on top of Jason Conrad-Bean's hand, holding it with both of his hands for a moment. "I am so sorry."

He let go of Jason Conrad-Bean's hand and turned to look at the lady. She was looking at him. As he reached out for her hand, she lunged at him and put her arms around her neck and she did start crying. "Oh, Obiad," she said between sobs.

"Anita," he said, as he awkwardly tried to pat her back as she cried on his shoulder. She was very beautiful, with long, flowing light brown hair and very large blue eyes.

She pushed away from my dad and turned to me. "This must be Layla? You look exactly the same, only different! You have grown up!" She gave me a big hug, squeezing me uncomfortably. "Where have you been all this time? Where did you grow up? Is this your boyfriend?" She pushed away from me and turned to Nadir.

Nadir smiled shyly and held out his hand. "I am Nadir," he said, not confirming or denying if he was my boyfriend. "It is very nice to meet you."

The men all turned to him and shook hands with him, then with me.

"How did you get here?" Wickersham asked.

Before we could answer, Salmoony asked, "Where have you been all this time?"

Anita said, "I can't believe you survived the air raid!"

"What is the matter with this thing?" Beezeeneck shouted. He looked as if he were about to toss the computer across the room.

I rushed over to him before he could throw it. "What's wrong?" I asked, trying to take it from him.

"This was the top-of-the-line, the latest technology, and although I can get it to do many of the most complicated tasks, it refuses to do something as simple as verify our location!" he shouted.

"Take it easy, Boss," Wickersham said. "What is it you have there?"

"It is the most sophisticated of the Zebra series computers, the Zebra-Zebra," Beezeeneck said, clearly frustrated. He handed the computer to Wickersham as Jason Conrad-Bean and Salmoony crowded around him to see it.

"It certainly is," Salmoony said. He got a big, goofy grin on his face. "Let me see it. Maybe I can get it to work." He held out his hand, but Wickersham was doing something to it.

"Hold on, I think I can fix it," Wickersham said.

I stepped away from them with the realization that I would have to go back and get another computer for myself, because it did not look like they were going to share with me. My ears perked up when I heard another conversation in the room.

"How did you and your daughter survive the air raid?" Anita was asking my dad. I thought she was standing a little too close to him. Even though we had known her nine years ago, she did not have the right to get in his personal space.

"The Bible saved my life."

She looked at him with her face all screwed up and he told her his story.

"As you know, I was working as a chaplain. We received an enormous shipment of Bibles, just two days before the air raid. I was to distribute them to anyone who wanted them. That morning, just a short time after I left home, I went into the warehouse. I was scheduled to work with several others to get the Bibles organized for distribution. I left Pierce in the office and as I was leaving, I heard him receiving his orders to fly out that morning. I was thinking about how thankful I was that I didn't have to go anywhere outside of the Four Quadrants.

"I went to the warehouse, but the other guys hadn't shown up yet. I started checking the stacks of boxes of Bibles by myself. I knew I wouldn't be able to do much until help arrived, because the boxes were huge, and they were stacked floor to ceiling. I was standing in the aisle, between the stacks of boxes, when I heard an explosion. It sounded like it was so close. I hit the floor, and I could hear more explosions, near and far, and I knew we were being bombed. I was lying there, between stacks of boxes of Bibles, and something hit the warehouse. I heard another explosion and even though I had my eyes shut tight, I saw a bright flash, like the sun had come and landed right beside me.

"The next thing I knew, it was deathly quiet. I

couldn't hear anything. I must have been knocked unconscious. As I opened my eyes, at first I couldn't see. I thought I had been blinded by the flash. Everything was dark. I checked to see if I was injured, and I didn't feel anything broken, but I was wedged underneath something and it was pitch black. I could smell an odor, something burning, so thick, but I couldn't move. I was stuck and I was blind. I didn't know what to do, so I fell asleep. I figured someone would come and help me get out.

"When I opened my eyes again, I could see. I had no idea how much time had passed. I still didn't hear anyone or anything. The atmosphere was so quiet. I could just smell awful odors, a terrible burning smell. I yelled out, as loud as I could, but nobody answered. Now I could see how the boxes had fallen and Bibles were stacked around me. The Word of God literally saved my life!"

"I am sure it did," Anita said, with a bad attitude in her voice.

"I discovered that I wasn't crushed, but I was able to move around a little. After moving little by little for a few hours, I finally got out from under the box of Bibles. They were all over, not stacked any more, but just all over, all around me. After I was finally able to stand up, I saw that everything in every direction was destroyed — everything but the Bibles. You know, the Bible says, 'heaven and earth will pass away, but the Word of God will stand forever.' "

"And you believe that?" Anita asked skeptically.

"With all my heart and all my mind," my dad said without hesitation.

The men's voices grew louder as they were arguing

around the computer.

"This should be working!" Salmoony shouted. "I know exactly how it works! I helped program these things!"

"Admit it, you've lost it," Wickersham said to him. "That was ten years ago that you worked on that project."

"Don't talk to me in that tone! I know what I am doing!" Salmoony's face got red as he pulled the computer away from Wickersham. "Let me see! Let me see it!" Salmoony insisted.

"Excuse me!" I shouted. Perhaps it was the shrill pitch of my voice or just the sheer volume, but everyone was suddenly quiet as they looked at me.

"I have an idea why it's not working," I said, quietly but firmly.

"How can you possibly have any idea of how it works?" Jason Conrad-Bean asked, as if I were just a baby. "You were only a child when these were programmed."

"Listen to what the kid has to say," Beezeeneck instructed, throwing his hands in the air, obviously frustrated with the whole situation.

"This whole area is blocked by some kind of mineral field or something," I said, remembering what Kenrick had told us about a type of electronic meltdown when we entered the valley where the Four Quadrants was. "When we came here, my two friends and me, none of our electronic devices would work once we came into the valley."

"The magnetism shield must have activated!" Beezeeneck and my dad said at the same time.

"That's it!" Salmoony agreed, nodding rapidly.

"That is why — " Wickersham began.

"That's why we never received any more communications from the expeditions!" Beezeeneck finished.

"This is why we have been able to communicate within the valley, inside the range of the shield, but nothing could cross over!" Salmoony explained, nodding his head with understanding.

This was exactly what I had been thinking for quite some time, but I hadn't known how to say it, or exactly what it was. I was rather pleased with myself for sharing this useful information, but they all ignored me as they began to make plans to turn off the shield.

While the adults were chattering excitedly and still holding on to my computer, I sat down on the couch to take a break. Things were happening so fast. I wondered if these guys would be able to communicate with the people at the Complex, or if they should even try.

Nadir sat beside me, close to me, inside my personal comfort zone.

"You are amazing," he said quietly, in a romantic voice. I felt chills and tinglies and I hoped I was not blushing. "You figured out what all the scientists did not know."

"I just put the pieces together," I said. "I just had a different perspective, that's all. That's what I do, or what I used to do, puzzles, put things together."

"And that is exactly what they needed," he said, leaning a little closer to me, so I could feel his breath on my neck.

"What about the others?" I said suddenly. "Do you think we should all be together?"

"I do not care about the others, as long as I am here with you," he whispered in my ear.

My heart skipped a beat and I tried to refocus my thoughts on the situation at hand, which was not my situation with Nadir, but getting all three groups together and making contact with the outside world.

I thought I should mention it to my dad, so the rest of our group could come and join us here in the lounge. I searched for him among the men, then noticed that he was being cornered across the room by Anita.

"I need to tell my dad something," I said, starting to get off the couch.

Nadir glanced in the direction of my dad and Anita. "He looks to be busy, do you not think?"

"I don't think—" I began, but he cut me off.

"Your father has not spoken to a woman in years," Nadir said quietly. "You can give him some privacy for a few minutes."

"But I don't want—"

He interrupted me again. "You do not want to be alone with me?"

He hit the nail right on the head, but I was not about to admit it.

"I just think it will be better when we all get together," I explained, "these guys and our people, all of us, together, so we are not all separated."

"We have plenty of time for that," Nadir said. "You have no reason to be afraid of me."

"I am not afraid of you," I began, but I didn't have an ending to the sentence. Yes, I was uncomfortable, but no, I did not really want to move away from Nadir. He had been so nice, so polite, so helpful, and he had shown a great deal more restraint than Jamal, and I liked him. So, what was my problem? I was not ready for this. I wanted to accomplish things in a logical manner and not stir up these strange feelings. Perhaps after living for nine years at the Complex, my own feelings had been more than controlled; they had been crushed. Still, I could not just jump into another mode immediately.

Nadir had an amused look on his face. I knew I should just relax. So many things had happened to me in such a short time. We were merely sitting together on a couch in a room full of people. I had nothing to fear.

I smiled at Nadir, hoping that my smile did not look like the expression of a crazy person, or of a frightened person.

"Okay," I said.

"Okay what?" he asked.

"I will just relax, here, now," I said, sighing.

"Am I too terrible?" he said.

"Oh, no, it's not that…"

"We can sit here and relax, now," he agreed.

Just then, Salmoony turned to me.

"What is this communication we are receiving?" he demanded. "The shield is still on!"

I jumped off the couch to look at the computer.

"It's just Lena," I said, boldly taking the computer from him. "Computer, videoconference with Lena."

"You can talk to it?" Wickersham asked. He seemed like one of those guys who was not interested in technology unless it could do something for him.

"It is voice-activated, and I have set it to recognize my voice," I explained, looking at the computer.

Lena's face popped up on the screen.

"I have something to tell you," I said to her.

"I have news for you," she said.

"You go first," I said, assuming that her news would be minor compared with my news.

"I want to say… can speak with Nadir?"

"Yes, sure, Nadir?" I turned to him as he was still sitting on the couch. "Lena wants to talk to you." I carried the computer over to him and he took it from me.

"Yes, Lena?"

She proceeded to speak to him in Arabic. I realized that she must have had a lot to say and did not want to struggle slowly with her English language. She began speaking rapidly, then it sounded like she was getting upset. She was talking for a few minutes and her voice began to escalate until she seemed to be yelling at Nadir. He spoke a few words to her and she was silent. He looked over the computer to speak to me.

"Tell your father to come," he said, then turned back to talk to Lena.

I quickly crossed the room, secretly happy to have a reason to break into the conversation between my dad and Anita. My dad looked over at me, and Anita turned her head to see who had stolen his attention away from her.

"Daddy, Nadir wants to tell you something. He just talked to Lena."

"Lena?" Anita practically shouted, looking at my dad. "Who is this Lena?" I thought Anita sounded jealous.

My dad sidestepped Anita without answering her and followed me to where Nadir was sitting. Anita followed close behind us and when my dad approached Nadir, Anita bumped into me. I just smiled at her and turned back to my dad and Nadir.

"What is it, son? What's going on?" my dad asked.

"I spoke with Lena. Some of the men go now back to the camp to get the elders. They are making decision, move here or stay at camp. They took with them one computer and lost contact. The men became very worried. I explain what Layla say about the magnetism and she explain to the rest so they now waiting for all to get together when others arrive."

I had a feeling he was leaving out some of the conversation, because nothing he had said would explain why Lena had sounded so angry, but it was not my place to say anything at this point.

My dad considered the information. "We will wait here and work on lowering the shield so we can make some external communication. When the rest of the group arrives in the other end of the shelter, we will invite them to come here and meet the ones who are here. Then we will all decide what to do."

"What to do about what?" I asked, feeling that our circumstances were about to change drastically.

Nadir was watching us intently, looking from me to my dad and back as we were talking. Anita was just standing there, staring at my dad.

"We will try to make contact, first with the ones who left here on the expeditions, then with anyone else who may have access to electronic communication," my dad said.

"Including the people at the Complex?" I asked. "Are you going to try to communicate with them?" One thing I did not want was for the State to decide our fate. Suppose I had to go back to the Complex and be punished? They would most likely send my dad out to one of the villages. I would prefer this simple life of wandering in the desert to the controlled, complex life at the Complex.

"We have not discussed that yet," my dad said. "We will probably try to contact them later, but our first priority is to try to contact the people who left here. We need to know if they are still alive, and if they are, where they are now."

"Maloof!" Salmoony yelled across the room.

My dad quickly left us to go see what Salmoony wanted. I followed him, a few steps behind him. Nadir followed me and Anita followed Nadir.

"We think we have deactivated the shield," Salmoony said, "but we need to get the cover closed before we can attempt any external communication."

"How can I help with that?" my dad asked.

"You, give me the computer," Salmoony demanded of Nadir. Nadir closed the videoconference window with a sweep of his palm across the screen and handed the computer to Salmoony.

"I can tap into the controls using this device and move the cover, but I need someone to go outside and physically look at the cover and be sure it is closing." He began typing commands into the computer.

"It has been open for more than nine years," my dad said.

"Exactly," Salmoony said, still typing, "so it might need some physical assistance. Can you and some of your men go outside? You can see if it is moving, and if necessary, you can give it a boost using the access levers. That will take four people."

"I was not made aware of the locations of the access levers," my dad said. "I was a chaplain, remember?"

"Okay, Wickersham can go with you," Salmoony instructed. "Take at least four other men with you, so you can have one on each lever and two extras in case any of the levers are stuck and need extra strength to get them moving."

"Did I hear you mention my name?" Wickersham asked, taking three long steps over to where our little group was standing.

"Yes, I need you to go with Maloof and a few others and show them where the access levers are for the magnetism shield."

"Outside?" Wickersham shouted. "I am NOT going outside! I'm not going to die out there!" He stomped his foot like a little kid.

"You are not going to die out there," Salmoony said in a soothing voice.

"Are you crazy? Everyone who has gone outside has not returned! They are all dead!" Wickersham said, still shouting.

I glanced around the room and saw that everyone

was staring at him.

"I am not going to commit suicide by leaving this place of safety," Wickersham said. "Salmoony, you go! Oh, I get it, you just want to get rid of me. You know the atmosphere outside is toxic."

"I am working on the controls," Salmoony said, still doing something with the computer.

"Well, I am not going to take a chance," Wickersham said, crossing his arms across his chest.

"We are not going to die if we go outside," my dad said calmly. "Look at me. I am not dead and I was out there ever since the bombings. The atmosphere is not toxic."

Wickersham looked at him skeptically.

"I was out there, too, and I am still alive," I said, hoping to encourage him.

"You are lying!" he shouted at me, and turned to my dad. "You have been hiding inside all this time, on the other side of the shelter, and you probably just came out of hiding because you ran out of food!"

"This is not true," Nadir said softly.

"I am not going to believe anything you say," Wickersham said to Nadir. "I don't even know who you are! What are you doing here, anyway?"

"He is part of a group of people who have kept me alive," my dad said, "outside, in the desert, for the last nine years."

"You would be dead if you were out there for nine minutes!" Wickersham shouted at my dad.

"He is not dead," I stated, "and he was out there all this time, until today."

"Obiad, I will go outside with you and help you," Nadir volunteered.

"I will go with you as well," Anita offered, giving my dad a provocative look.

"You are not going anywhere," Wickersham said to Anita as he grabbed her arm.

She pulled away from his grip. "You don't tell me what to do. You are not my boss. I can go outside if I want to, and I want to."

"I will take Nadir and three others who came with me," my dad said, "but I need to take someone who knows where to find the levers. By now they are probably buried deep beneath the sand drifts."

"I want to go outside," Anita whined.

"You can go outside if you want," Salmoony said with a sigh. I got the feeling he was tired of her whining. I was tired of it and I had only been around her for a few minutes. He had been locked up in this place with her for nine years!

"Yeah, you can go outside and DIE!" Wickersham shouted at Anita.

Beezeeneck, who apparently had been out of the room, came to see what the fuss was all about.

"What is going on here? What's your problem, Wickersham?" he said with an authoritative tone to his voice. He put his face right in front of Wickersham's face.

"I am not going to go outside and die!" Wickersham insisted.

"No one is forcing you to go outside," Beezeeneck said patronizingly, taking a slight step away from him.

"We need someone to go with Maloof and a few of his men to show them where the access levers are for the magnetism shield," Salmoony explained. "The shield has been deactivated, but we don't have visual access to see if the cover has been raised. Maloof doesn't know where they levers are located."

"Quit your crying, Wickersham," Beezeeneck said.

"We have stayed alive all this time because we have been in here," Wickersham said. "I am not about to throw that all away just because Mooney tells me to go outside."

"So, don't go," Beezeeneck said. "I'll go with you, Obiad. Wickersham, you do whatever Salmoony needs you to do. Salmoony, keep him inside with you."

"Yes, sir," Wickersham said, with a look of satisfaction on his face.

"I, on the other hand, am anxious to go outside!" Beezeeneck said, rubbing the palms of his hands together. "What are we waiting for?"

"Yes, what are we waiting for?" Anita repeated. She had a big, silly smile on her face.

"Can we use the computer to navigate back to the far west entrance?" my dad asked Salmoony.

"Oh, no need," Beezeeneck said. "We can go out the central entrance, just down the hall."

"But we need to get a few more men, and they are at the other end," my dad explained.

Beezeeneck nodded. "We will not need to use the computer. Just follow me. What else have I had to do for nine years besides memorize this underground maze? I feel like a trained rat, and now I am ready to get out of this cage!"

"Layla, you come with us, and you can lead the others back here," my dad said. He turned to Beezeeneck. "Or is this the best place to meet? We will have a total of twenty-five people, once the others arrive."

"Yeah, this is a good place to meet. Then we can set up living arrangements. We have plenty of bunks for all to stay."

Everyone was buzzing with excitement as we left the room. Beezeeneck distributed flashlights to each of us and led the way with my dad behind him. Anita followed closely behind my dad. I could hear her babbling about something. I stayed more than a few steps behind Anita — something about her odor bothered me — and Nadir was right behind me, close enough for him to frequently put his hand on my shoulder or my waist.

"Much excitement we have today," Nadir said.

"Yes, isn't it?" I asked.

"You change our lives," he said, resting his hand on my shoulder as we went around a corner.

"My life is completely different, too," I said, trying to downplay the importance of his statement.

"I now wear Western clothing!" he said, "all because of you."

I smiled, but I knew he could not see my face. What we had called 'Western clothing' were those old cowboy hats and leather outfits. I had never thought of mere pants and shirts as being Western clothing, but, I supposed, to these people from an Eastern area of the world, they were. Nadir did look a lot more attractive in regular clothing than he had in that robe. As a matter of fact, all of the men from my dad's village looked better in pants than they had in robes.

"You brought us here, to this place, and brought computers into our life," Nadir continued.

"I didn't do all of that," I said, as we wound around a series of corners.

"Before you come to us, our life the same every day," Nadir said. "We wear same robe, we eat same food, we sleep in same tent, we see same people. Now all for us is new, because of you. You change everything for us. You upgrade our life."

I had not considered all of that; I just wanted to be with my dad and have a good life with him.

"You are very kind to say that," I said.

"YOU are very kind to us," he replied.

I was very thankful to end this conversation when we finally reached the door to the other room where some of the villagers were waiting. Lena and Salwa seemed especially happy to see Nadir, but he pushed past them to address the native Arabic speakers and explain to them what was happening. He and three other men, along with Jamal, Beezeeneck and Anita, immediately left to go take care of the shield situation. They took one of the computers with them so they could communicate with us and with Salmoony.

For some reason, Lena and Salwa were not acting as friendly to me as they had been before, and I felt a little anxious when my dad left me there with them. All I wanted was to be with him. I did not really care if the cover to the shield was up or down, or if we could communicate with anyone outside of this place. As far as I could see, we had everything we needed right here. We could live in this shelter place very comfortably and we could go outside for fresh air or to hunt and gather whatever they hunted and gathered on their hunting and gathering trips.

I sat in one of the chairs apart from the rest of the group. As I put my hand on the arm rest, I felt some buttons under my fingers. Without thinking about it, I pushed one button and the wall in front of me dissolved into a screen, a large monitor. I pushed the same button again before I could get into any trouble for messing around with things, and a movie started to play on the screen. The rest of the group gathered around me and sat in nearby chairs.

This program appeared to be an introduction to living in the shelter. The first part of the movie was about rules and safety inside the shelter. It showed a map of the exits and the where the emergency equipment was located in each pod. Next, it went into the location of the food and shower rooms, where the clothing and linens were located, and where the occupants were to report for their assignments. Finally, it showed where the exercise and entertainment rooms were, including several movie theaters, music and dance rooms, libraries, computer labs, and virtual gaming rooms.

Although the shelter had been built to house more than a thousand people, I did not see where they had considered that children might be among them. What had they planned for children to do who were confined to this shelter? Or had it been planned only for adults? That was a scary thought, that the leaders of our society had not looked ahead to a time when children might have needed to live here.

As soon as the movie ended, the men began to talk excitedly. Since they were not speaking in English, I didn't know what they were saying. I wondered if they were more excited about the new variety of food, the opportunity to listen to music, or to be able to play a virtual game. They all ignored me and did not clue me in to what they were talking about, so I just sat in the chair and waited.

I must have fallen asleep, because before I knew it, the ones who had gone to take care of the shield were back in the room. I didn't see my dad, so I went over to Nadir to ask him where he was.

"I have some bad news for you," he said solemnly.

Oh, no, oh, no, I thought. I did not want to hear any bad news about my dad.

"What?" I demanded. "Where is he? Is he okay?" I searched the room more closely to see if I had overlooked him.

"He has injury," Nadir said. He then said something loudly in Arabic, and I assumed he was telling everyone else what had happened.

"Where is he? I asked again. "Please take me to him!"

"Beezeeneck taking him to doctor," Nadir said. "I think he will be okay."

"Taking him to a doctor?" I asked, aware that my voice was rising. "Where—"

"The man we meet, Mr. Conrad-Bean, is doctor," he explained.

"Doctor Conrad-Bean?" I asked, shaking my head. I was still trying to figure out what was going on with my dad.

"That is correct," Nadir said.

"Well, let's go!" I said, pulling Nadir by the hand as I headed for the door.

"You leave us again?" Lena asked anxiously.

"Stay and wait," Nadir told her, as I pulled him into the hallway.

We rushed down one hallway and into the next. I was thankful I had clipped the flashlight to the strap on my pants, otherwise we would have been travelling in darkness. We turned one corner, then another, then another and we came to a dead end, a hallway with one locked door.

"This isn't the right way!" I cried.

"We go back and turn to right instead of left," Nadir suggested.

"No, I think we need to go back two turns," I said, trying hard to remember our way. We had no computer to guide us and our memories were failing us in this matter.

I started to go back when Nadir grabbed my hand.

"No need to go fast," he said, pulling me toward him.

"I have to see my dad!"

"His injury not bad," he said. "He, how you say it, smash his hand. Not serious."

"He smashed his hand?" I asked. "That IS serious!"

"No, I am serious," he said, and I could see a sparkle in his eye in the light of the flashlight. "I am serious of you."

"We don't have time for that now," I said, not wanting this to be happening, and not wanting to delay finding where my dad was. "Let's go back and get one of the computers so we can find where he is."

"I know the way," Nadir said quietly.

"Well, then, let's go!"

He pulled me close to him and leaned down to me, so our faces were nearly touching.

"You would like to be my wife?" he asked, wrapping his other arm around me.

"No, I mean, not now, I mean, I just want to find my dad!" This whole situation was frustrating to me.

"You want to wait for later?" he asked slyly.

"I do not even want to have this discussion now!" I tried to pull away from him, but he was very strong.

"I have very patient," he said. "We can discuss later."

He let me go and I ran down the hallway, almost frantic. When I reached a fork in the hallway, I stopped, and he ran into my back. I hadn't realized he was so close to me, but there he was again, right with me.

"Which way?" I asked. I was truly turned around with nothing to indicate which way we should go.

"Go to the left," he said.

"But did we come that way?" I asked.

"We go that way," he said with confidence, so I turned to the left. Each time we came to another crossroad, Nadir calmly told me which way to go until, finally, we stepped into the lounge where we had been before.

"Where's my dad?" I demanded, looking around the room. Wickersham was the only person in there.

"How should I know?" he snapped. "I am just doing my job."

"And that would be?" I asked. I did not really care what his job was, but he was just irritating me and I wanted some answers. I needed to find my dad!

"She mean to say, where we can find Dr. Conrad-Bean?"

"The DOCTOR is in his OFFICE," Wickersham said rudely. He turned his head away from us.

"And where is that office?" Nadir asked. I was impressed by how well he was keeping his cool.

"Go out, to the right, two doors down on the left," Wickersham said, suddenly sounding as if he were so bored. He waved his hand at us, shooing us away.

We left Wickersham and followed his directions. I gently pushed open the door to the doctor's office with Nadir right behind me. I was not at all prepared for what I saw.

CHAPTER 7

The room was stark and all the walls and cabinets were shiny silver. My dad was sitting on a chair, holding his left arm with his right hand. His left hand looked to be mangled; smashed, fingers going in all directions, with blood all over the place. I tried to gasp, but no sound came out because Nadir had clapped his hand over my mouth. My stomach did a flip-flop and I felt faint. I leaned against Nadir for support as we stood in the doorway, frozen and unnoticed, while Dr. Conrad-Bean lowered a silver pyramid over my dad's hand.

My dad sat back in the chair and closed his eyes. Dr. Conrad-Bean waved one of his hands over the silver pyramid and it began to shine, to glow. The reflection off the silver was so intense I had to squint my eyes into slits. I could hear a strange sound, something like the sound of a ball rolling around in a metal bowl only much louder. The light and the sound grew more intense.

My dad let out a "Ya!" and I had the sickening feeling that the doctor had just cut off my dad's hand.

The sound slowly got more quiet, the glow began to fade, and when the bright and noisy device was back to being a simple silver pyramid, my dad opened his eyes. Dr. Conrad-Bean lifted the pyramid, looked closely at the hand, and my dad smiled. My eyes were still affected by the bright reflection and I blinked them in disbelief. My dad's hand was completely normal again! There was no blood, the hand did not look crushed, and even every fingernail was in perfect condition. My dad's hand was like new!

"How did you do that?" I asked, pushing my way into the doctor's office.

"Where did you come from?" Anita asked, entering the room from a side door. Beezeeneck followed her into the room.

I ignored her because I didn't feel like her question needed an answer. She knew where I had been.

"Daddy, your hand!" I exclaimed. "What happened? How did that thing fix it?"

"I merely used our rapid regeneration pyramid," Dr. Conrad-Bean said as he held the pyramid up near one of the silver cabinets. The front of the cabinet looked as if it turned into liquid, kind of shimmering. The pyramid was kind of sucked into the watery appearance and disappeared as the cabinet again returned to its solid state. I was staring at the cabinet, blinking hard, trying to believe what my eyes had just seen.

"That is amazing," Nadir said, stepping around me. He apparently hadn't been looking at the cabinet trick, but at my dad. He went over to my dad to get a closer look at his hand. "Amazing," he repeated.

"I have had lots of time to work on it and to perfect it, but not many opportunities to put it to use," Dr. Conrad-Bean said. He turned to the sink and washed his hands.

"How does it feel?" I asked my dad.

"I'm not sure my brain realizes that my hand is completely healed," he said. "I hardly believe it, and I am looking right at it. I saw it happen. Seems to be in working condition." He wiggled his fingers and looked at the back of his hand, then at his palm.

"You may still be in shock from the accident," Dr. Conrad-Bean said, turning to face my dad. "Just tell yourself that your hand is no longer injured and you are whole again. Eventually, your mind and the rest of your body will understand that you are healed. You must do this to prevent retaining a phantom injury, which is an injury you no longer have but your mind has yet to accept the fact that your body is healed. By consciously telling yourself that you are healed and whole, you speed up the process of your mind accepting the fact. Keep telling yourself, over and over, that you are completely healed."

"It seems to be working properly," my dad said, still inspecting it.

"We didn't have anything like this back at the Complex," I said.

"It was only available for military testing until the air raids," Dr. Conrad-Bean said. "Like I said, I had plenty of time to work on it and perfect it since then. As you can see, it is working properly now."

"Yeah, finally," Anita added. She added something to her tone of voice that I did not like. "It is about time."

"I have to admit," Dr. Conrad-Bean said, "you, Obiad, have been the biggest success I have had. Of course, we haven't had many accidents down here."

"I can tell you one thing," Anita said, "your fancy-schmancy silver cone thing can NOT bring a person back from the dead."

"That is not the purpose," Dr. Conrad-Bean said. "It is to be used to heal the living. That is what I have done. See for yourself." He stepped away from my dad to allow Anita room to stand by him. "By the way, it is a pyramid, not a cone."

Dr. Conrad-Bean and Anita exchanged evil glances and I was sure there was more to their story than they were telling us, but that didn't matter to me. I was back with my dad again, and he was fine now.

"What does a fellow have to do to get something to eat around here?" my dad asked, looking around the room, as if some treat were going to pop out of the wall, or maybe all those silver walls were actually refrigerator doors.

I was suddenly very hungry, reminded about food.

Beezeeneck stepped over to my dad. "We are preparing breakfast for all," he said proudly.

"Breakfast?" I asked. I really had no idea what time it was, and since I had not been out of this underground shelter for such a long time, I had no idea if it were dark or light. It seemed to me that days had gone by since we climbed down that ladder.

"Yes, it will soon be zero seven hundred," Beezeeneck said. "We thought we would wait for the rest of Maloof's troop to arrive."

"I doubt that they will be here any time soon," my dad said. "Our camp is really quite a distance away from here."

"Did you call them on the computer?" I asked.

"Ah, yes, I will have Salmoony call them and check on the progress," Beezeeneck said, nodding his head.

"Please excuse me, sir, I should be there for the translation?" Nadir asked.

"Naw, he can just use the automatic translator," Beezeeneck said. "Salmoony will speak in English and they, whoever is on the other end, will hear them in their language, whatever that is."

"That is very nice," Nadir said, but I was getting the

feeling he was rather disappointed at not being needed for this task. I, on the other hand, was very impressed with this feature.

"Thank you, Dr. Conrad-Bean," my dad said, still examining his healed hand.

"Just doing my job, Maloof," he replied.

"Let's get out of here and go back to the lounge, or we can go to the mess hall," Beezeeneck said.

"Mess hall?" Nadir asked, confused. "You have a hall for your mess?"

I was glad he asked, because I did not want to appear ignorant.

My dad and Beezeeneck chuckled.

"Cafeteria, eatery, the place with all the food," Anita said with a little impatience.

"Before we go, I would like to offer up a prayer of thanksgiving," my dad said. Since he was the chaplain, the others all froze in place, waiting for him to pray.

"Let us join hands," my dad suggested.

Anita practically leaped into position to be one holding my dad's hand. I gently took his other hand, the one which was newly restored (and it felt brand new, smooth and warm) and Nadir took my other hand. We stood in a circle and I closed my eyes as my dad thanked God.

"Lord, I thank You today for Your goodness and Your mercy. I thank You for Your healing power and for giving the wisdom to this doctor to use the technology, which could not have been invented if You had not given us a mind to think. I thank You for the miracle of a perfectly new hand, a hand which now feels no pain, not even the slightest bit of discomfort. I thank You for bringing us together on this day, and I thank You for what You have already done, for what You are doing right now, and what You are going to do. Let us glorify You with everything we do. In the name of Your precious son, Jesus, we pray. Amen."

"Amen," the rest of us said.

As I opened my eyes, I thought I saw the remnant of a smirk on Anita's face. She had some weird spirit about her and I didn't really like it, but at this point, I couldn't do anything about it, so I just let it go.

We left the doctor's office and went back to the lounge where Salmoony and Wickersham were wearing these kind of strange, puffy suits, and I realized they were playing a virtual game. A holographic image of two robots or monsters across the room was replicating every movement of theirs. They punched and jumped and danced around each other, and the images, glimmering in bright greens and blues and purples, did whatever the two men were doing. I wanted to laugh because the whole thing seemed ridiculous to me, but what else did they have to do to pass the time, the days, the weeks, the months, the years underground, with only a few other people to interact with? Even a doctor could only perfect so many healing pyramids. He would have to have some kind of distraction, some kind of fun exercise to pass the time.

We watched them with amusement (or, in my case, bored amusement, because after about a minute, the game was no longer fascinating to watch) for awhile before Beezeeneck interrupted them to ask Salmoony where he had put the computer. Salmoony pulled it out from inside the puffy suit and handed it to Beezeeneck.

"This is headquarters to the expedition," he said, after he opened the videoconference screen. He spoke to them for a few minutes, and everything they said came across in a computerized voice in English, which was very impressive.

I was not giving him my full attention because I was distracted by the way Anita appeared to be flirting with my dad. The funny thing was, my dad did not seem to notice that she was acting like a teenager — a young, immature teenager. He just kept talking, answering her questions honestly and he did not fall into her little traps.

"Okay, we can go ahead and eat," Beezeeneck announced. "The rest of Maloof's troop won't be back until much later. Let's head to the mess hall."

We followed him to another room, which was large and silver and bare. I had a feeling these rooms had been designed by an engineer and not an architect, because they were merely functional and not at all inviting. However, I could smell a trace of food cooking, and the scent served to take my mind off the starkness and coldness of the room.

As we entered the room, the lights slowly warmed, giving the room a more pleasant atmosphere. I was third in line, behind my dad and in front of Anita, and I stopped in my tracks when silver tables and benches just came up from the floor. Anita bumped into me, but I was entranced by the transformation of the room. On the tables, cloth napkins with sets of silverware appeared. I began walking again when I noticed the gap between my dad and myself had grown. I caught up with him and followed the lead of Beezeeneck and my dad. A list of foods appeared in red lettering a little farther down the line.

Beezeeneck said, "Eggs, toast, bacon, orange juice," and moved a couple of feet to his left. A plate with eggs, toast and bacon appeared and he took it. He took another step sideways and a glass with his orange juice appeared. He grabbed it and moved out of the line, over to a table.

My dad ordered the same thing, plus coffee, and I watched in fascination as the plate with the food appeared, seeming to float in the air, and my dad took it. He put his glass of orange juice on the plate so he could take the cup of coffee with his other hand, and he walked over to the table and sat across from Beezeeneck.

I was stunned. Anita nudged me and I automatically said, "Eggs, toast, bacon, orange juice," grabbed my plate, and moved to my left, just as the men before me had done. My glass of orange juice appeared and I went to sit beside my dad. I felt as if I were in a dream, because these kinds of things just did not happen. Food did not appear upon demand and objects did not float in the air while waiting for a human to pluck them.

Anita claimed her spot on the other side of my dad, and the others quickly went through the line. Nadir sat beside me on the other side. I was waiting for the others to start eating, and as soon as everyone was seated around the table, my dad said the blessing. I was expecting my egg to be cold by the time we ate, but when I tasted it, I was surprised that it was still warm, the perfect temperature. I was also surprised that it was real, that I was not dreaming, because I could taste it and feel it in my mouth.

My dad instinctively knew what I was thinking, or at least part of it.

"These plates were made from the amalgamation, were they not?" my dad asked Beezeeneck, as he took a bite of his toast.

"Yes, and they keep our food at the same temperature as it is when it touches the plate," Beezeeneck said.

"What is hot stays hot and what is cold stays cold," Anita said, matter-of-factly.

"I like this, what you call it, amaga—?" Nadir said, tapping his plate with a fork.

"Amalgamation, a fusion of substances," Dr. Conrad-Bean explained, chewing furiously. I noticed that his plate was loaded with food, and also, his plate was much larger than the rest of ours.

"Where did this food come from?" I asked. "I mean, was it vacuum sealed ever since the Before Time?"

Dr. Conrad-Bean and Beezeeneck shook their heads, but did not answer, I assumed, because their mouths were full.

"We grow our food and animals for our consumption," Wickersham said, licking his fingers. "We have, I guess you would call it, an underground farm. We can go and look at it later, if you want to see it."

"I do!" I said, taking my last bite of food. I picked up my glass of orange juice and drank it all at one time. This meal was so tasty!

"That would be kind of interesting," my dad said, taking a sip of his coffee. "Oh, that's good," he said, setting his cup on the table. "I haven't had coffee in years," he remarked.

Salmoony, who was sitting at the far end of the table,

suddenly slapped his leg. He had not even touched his food.

"Incredible!" he shouted, looking at the computer.

"What is it?" Beezeeneck asked, getting out of his seat to join Salmoony.

"We have made contact!" Salmoony said. "Oh, this is classified."

He stood up from the table and quickly left the room. Beezeeneck, Dr. Conrad-Bean and Wickersham followed him. Anita stayed beside my dad, who was shaking his head.

"What are they talking about?" I asked. "We have been in contact with the others all this time."

"I think he meant that we have made contact with someone in the outside world," my dad said.

"Of course that is what he means, Sweetie," Anita said, as if my statement had been made by a two-year-old. "How could you possibly think he meant anything else?"

"My thought was the same as your thought," Nadir said to me. I was not sure if he really meant that or he was just trying to make me feel better, but, in any case, I did feel a little bit better, and less childish. At least I was not acting childish like Anita was.

"You three stay here while I go check into this situation," my dad said, standing up.

"I will go with you," Anita said, leaping to her feet.

"No, you stay here with Layla and Nadir," my dad instructed as he headed for the door.

"I have every right to know what is going on," Anita said, sticking out her lower lip. She really was a baby.

"You will know, soon enough," my dad said calmly. "I need you to stay here with these two young people."

"Oh, I get it, a chaperone," she said, nodding her head dramatically. "We cannot leave the two young lovers alone now, can we?"

"That is not what I meant," my dad said, standing at the door. "We don't know our way around here, so, please, just stay here with them until I come back. I will only be gone for a few minutes."

"We can just watch them on the monitors," Anita said, winking at my dad. "We have cameras everywhere, you know."

That thought had not crossed my mind, but I had to admit, it was a good possibility.

"No, I would like for you to stay here with them," my dad clarified.

"Well, when you put it that way," Anita said. "I will do anything you like, even if I have to stay here and babysit."

"Thank you," my dad said, dropping the conversation so he could leave. He disappeared through the doorway.

He instantly came back into the room.

"I have no idea where they went," he announced with a smile. He came back into the room and was about to sit on the bench.

A few seconds later, before my dad could even sit down, Wickersham came into the room.

"Maloof, you come with me," he said, turned, and went out the door.

My dad followed him and the door closed behind

them.

I was about to remark that we could do the clean-up duty. I figured Anita would show us where to put everything, and maybe we would see some more advanced technology at work. As I opened my mouth to speak, my empty plate and my glass dissolved into the table. As I watched, every empty plate and glass did the same thing, one at a time. They just seemed to melt into the table top. My dad's coffee cup, Nadir's glass of milk and Salmoony's plate and glass all remained. I guessed that was because they were not empty. Well, there went clean-up duty.

"The system is set for automatic clean-up," Anita explained in a bored tone of voice. "As soon as the majority of the plates are empty, they are automatically removed from the table."

"Where do they go?" I asked. I immediately wished I had not said that, because Anita already thought I didn't have a brain.

"Where do you think they go?" she asked, rolling her eyes.

"Oh, yeah, of course," I said, and, of course, I didn't know. I saw them go into the table, so I had to assume they were collected, cleaned and sterilized and put back into the stack of clean plates, glasses and silverware.

"Yes, of course," Nadir repeated. I looked at him and he gave me a kind smile. I realized he and I were in the same boat, and probably it didn't matter if we did not know where the dishes went.

My dad came back into the room, startling me.

"I think we should go back to where the others are and get some sleep," he said. "We have been up for too many hours and we may have a big task ahead of us."

"What?" Anita demanded. "What are we going to do?"

"Well, you can make your own decision, but I would like Layla and Nadir to get some sleep, along with the others who came here with us," my dad said. "We will talk about it after we have gotten some rest. Come on."

He turned and went out of the room. I was not about to lose sight of him, so I scrambled to catch up with him. Nadir and Anita quickly followed.

"Do you remember the way back to the beginning, Daddy?" I asked.

"Salmoony has lit up our pathway using green lighting so we won't get lost," my dad said.

I had not noticed before he mentioned it, but the hallway was lit in a dim green. As we hurried along the corridors, we were able to stay on track by going where it was green. Other hallways were now lit in red, so we knew to not go any other way.

"What is going on?" Anita shouted at my dad. She was stuck behind Nadir, who was behind me, so she was not able at this moment to catch up to my dad.

My dad either did not hear her or he chose to ignore her question. He just kept moving quickly and I stayed right with him.

When we finally reached the others, we found some of them were already asleep. Salwa was stretched out on a couch, a few others were sleeping on couches and chairs, but Lena was talking on the computer to the group of men who were on their way to join us.

"They shall arrive in one or two hours," she

announced with a smile, when she saw us coming into the room.

"We need to get some rest before they arrive," my dad said. Nadir repeated it in Arabic, and the men nodded and found places to lie down.

Anita walked over to one of the walls and waved her hand. Several more couches came out of the wall as if they were coming through water, but they were not wet. Now everyone had a place to rest, and I settled on the opposite end of the couch of where my dad was. The couch was nice and large, so we did not end up kicking each other. Anita sat in a chair, apparently not ready to take a nap, but I snuggled into the softness of the couch as it warmed to my body and seemed to wrap itself around me. I did not even need a blanket. The room became quiet and I was asleep within a few seconds.

When I opened my eyes, seemingly just a moment later, the room was abuzz with activity. Most of the couches had been removed from the room and men were talking and gesturing. My dad was already awake, sitting at his end of our couch and using a computer. As I looked around the room, I noticed that everyone had his own computer. I saw the crate that had held the computers sitting in one corner. Lena was asleep while sitting in a chair with her head on the table, and her dad was right beside her, also sleeping with his head on the table. The rest of the group was awake and learning about the computers. Nadir and Jamal were standing not too far from me, both doing something with their computers, comparing, discussing, learning together.

My dad looked up from his computer and saw that I was awake.

"Here is your computer, my darling daughter," he

said, handing one to me. I hoped for an instant that it was the one I had already set up, but when I turned it on, it started at the beginning. I went through the set-up process on this computer and soon it was ready for my use. Nadir and I set ours to be able to videoconference, and then my dad and I did the same. My dad went around the room and set up everyone else to be able to contact him. When he came back to the couch, he showed me that he had acquired little pictures of each person, and all he had to do was either say a name or touch a picture to initiate a conversation with that person, or a group of people.

"Can everyone please be seated?" Beezeeneck said loudly. "Please, sit down, we have an announcement to make."

Nadir went up to him and offered to translate for him, but Beezeeneck told him they would be using their computers for translation. Nadir came and sat on the couch beside me. I was expecting Anita to squeeze in on the end near my dad, but she was nowhere in sight. The men and boys took their seats. By this time, Lena and her father were awake, and we all waited to hear the announcement.

"We have had some communication from the outside world," Beezeeneck began.

By the look on his face, I was afraid he was going to say something about the Complex. I heard the faint translation of his sentence on some of the computers.

"Our people, some of those who left here, are living some distance away from here. They were as surprised to hear from us as we were to hear from them. They assumed we were dead, just as we had assumed they were dead. However, they are alive, at least some of them are."

"What about Uncle Pierce?" I whispered to my dad.

"Shh, listen," he said.

"We have a decision to make," Beezeeneck continued. "Do we want to stay here, where we know we have food, shelter and protection from the weather, and now, the opportunity to go outside as often as we desire? Or do we want to make the trek to the other location where, from all reports, more than one thousand people are living?"

The room burst into discussion in two languages, so loud I thought my ears were going to suffer permanent damage.

"Hold it, hold it!" Beezeeneck shouted. "We need to weigh the pros and cons. Also, we do not have to make a decision immediately. However, if we do decide to go, we have quite a distance to cover on foot, perhaps a hundred miles or so. The terrain may be rough in some areas, and we can never be sure about the weather.

"If we decide to stay, we can get more comfortable with our computers and we can communicate with the others until we decide to go. We can wait for them to come and pick us up, as they have said they have transport vehicles. The decision is ours.

"Take a few minutes to discuss the matter amongst yourselves, and then we can discuss it some more as a group."

"What do you think, Daddy?" I asked, filtering out all the other conversations in the room.

"I really do not have a preference," my dad said, "as long as I stay with you."

"Me too," I said. "This is a pretty neat place." I thought about the delicious, fresh food and the opportunity to see an underground farm and the dissolving walls.

"It is certainly an upgrade to the way I have been living," my dad said with a chortle.

I noticed that Anita was standing by Wickersham, who was jabbering in her ear, but she was not paying any attention to him. She was focused on what my dad was saying.

"Do you see any reason why we should leave here?" I asked. "I mean, now? We could stay for awhile and then go, if we decide to go. This place has everything we need, for now, anyway."

"Well, there is just one thing to think about," my dad said, putting a strand of my hair behind my ear. "Pierce may be there, at the other place."

"I would love to see him again," I admitted, "but we could wait awhile and relax and enjoy ourselves here."

"Yes, we could do that," my dad said, nodding.

"Do you feel like we could walk all that way?" I asked. I was afraid to admit that I was not really in the best physical shape. Exercising for an hour or two each day had not at all prepared me for living in the outside world. Besides, I had only had one shower since I left Complex, and I had been in the habit of having at least one shower every day.

"Maybe we could communicate with the ones at the other place, I guess it's a city or large community, and see if we can locate Uncle Pierce. Then if we find him, we can go there. Or he can come here." I nodded my head to confirm that this was probably the best decision.

"Because of the distance, you and I cannot plan to go on our own. We would have to travel with a group, so we could carry the supplies we need to go that distance. So if we decide to go, we have to go when others are also ready to go."

"Okay," I said, with a good answer ready. "We can stay here for awhile, get rested up, try to contact Uncle Pierce, and whenever the next group is ready to go, we can go with them."

"I'll tell you what let's do," my dad suggested, and I could hear some kind of compromise coming. "Let's see how soon the group will leave. Maybe they will want to wait for a month or so, and I think that would be enough time for us to get ready to go with them."

"That sounds good," I said, really hoping they would want to stay here for at least six months.

"Attention, everyone!" Beezeeneck shouted.

The noise in the room immediately stopped and we all turned to look at him.

"Do we have any volunteers who want to leave?" he asked.

"I, for one, am not leaving the safety of this place to go to some unknown place just because someone said something else is out there," Wickersham said.

"Thank you, Wickersham," Beezeeneck said. "You are entitled to your own choice. Now, I don't need to hear from everyone who is wanting to stay here. I am asking about those who want to go."

The room was silent. I could imagine that the men and children from my dad's tribe were looking at this shelter as a type of utopia, with everything they needed right at hand, so it was no wonder that they wanted to stay. However, I thought at least some of the military people would be adventurous, hoping to get out of this giant underground box to the world above.

Anita was looking at my dad, waiting to see if he was going to say anything.

"I would like to go," Salmoony said, stepping to the front of the crowd. He turned toward us. "I am ready to get out of here and see what is happening in the rest of the world."

"Good for you, Salmoony," Beezeeneck said. "Anyone else?"

"Plus, I would have a much better chance of finding a wife there than here," Salmoony added.

Everyone laughed, but really, it wasn't funny. That statement was true. Anita was the only woman here, and Lena, Salwa and I were the only girls, so even if he waited for us to grow up, he would have to compete with all the other men here, twenty-five in all.

"I will be better off without a silly woman in my life," Wickersham announced, throwing an evil look in Anita's direction.

"I am sure you will, Wickersham," Beezeeneck said.

Lena's dad stepped forward. "I will go," he said, "and my daughter with me."

"Okay, we have three," Beezeeneck said. "We need five, at the minimum, in order to carry all the supplies you will need for the journey. Do we have two more?"

"How soon are you planning to leave?" my dad asked, causing my heart to skip a beat. For an instant, I thought he was also volunteering to go.

"As soon as we can get our supplies together," Salmoony said. "I see no reason to delay."

"How long will that take?" I asked. Everyone looked at me and I smiled weakly.

"I expect we can leave bright and early this evening, after we get a good day's sleep," Salmoony said.

"This evening?" I asked, surprised. I thought it would take at least a week to gather things for a trip on foot of a hundred miles or more.

"Yep," Salmoony said. "That is, if we can get at least two more to come with us."

I saw Salwa talking to her father, and I suspected she wanted to go since Lena was going. Her father was shaking his head.

"*Baba*!" Salwa cried, but to no avail. He turned away from her.

"Anyone?" Beezeeneck asked.

The crowd remained silent as he looked around the room.

"I am prepared to go," Beezeeneck finally said with a sigh. "Well, what we can do, we can gather supplies together, enough for five or seven people, and we will be ready to go as soon as we get one more volunteer. We just need one more. Do we have one more?"

I looked at my dad, but I saw with satisfaction that he was staying with our decision. I felt like I could just say, yes, we would go, and we would go, but I did not want to leave this comfortable home yet. I was ready to take another shower, and as soon as I could, I would.

"We can use the glider carts," Salmoony said suddenly, raising a finger in the air.

"They are buried under —" Wickersham began.

"No! Salmoony is right!" Beezeeneck said. "We can

dig them out! They were in storage, right beside where the computers were!"

"What's a glider cart?" I asked.

"That is what I would like to know," my dad said.

"They glide above the sand," Salmoony explained. "We can put all our supplies in them. We were preparing them for use back before the air raids, and we had them stored. All they need is a day in the sun to charge up."

"So, we can go with just four of us," Beezeeneck said, "even if one is a young woman. Come, let us work on digging out one or two of them to take with us."

"Can we ride in them?" I asked, as a large group moved toward the door. My dad started to go out, so I did, too.

Beezeeneck laughed. "You might be able to ride in one, but if I were to get in one, it would never get off the ground. We were working on making them capable of bearing more weight, but we were not there yet."

We went down the hallway and the ladder came into view. As soon as Beezeeneck opened the door to the outside, sunlight came streaming in, hurting my eyes. In just this short time underground, my eyes had become accustomed to the dimness of being inside. The brightness was giving my eyes physical pain, so I squinted hard, making my eyes into tiny slits.

"It is already quite hot out here," Beezeeneck announced, as he fanned his face with his hand.

As soon as I climbed out of the hole, I felt the heat on my head, but, strangely enough, not on my body. I figured the outfit was somehow weather-proof. I just needed a hat, because the sun's rays were like fire on the top of my head.

"Let me help you," Dr. Conrad-Bean said, stepping over to me. He was wearing a hood, and I saw that Beezeeneck and Anita were also wearing them. Dr. Conrad-Bean reached over to my shoulder and pulled a hood out of nowhere, which is to say, out of the neckline of my shirt. My head was instantly cool. The other men who were newly changed out of robes into 'Western' wear, followed his example and pulled hoods out of their shirts and over their heads.

Not everyone had come out to help with the digging, and I assumed some were already gathering supplies for the voyage. My dad was already down in the hole, helping with the digging. I stepped away from the activity so I would not be in the way. Although it was nice to be outside and breathing fresh air again, I really wanted to go back inside and take another nap.

Nadir came over to me, and I saw Lena eyeing him suspiciously. I started to think that maybe they were somehow involved with each other. Or was she upset because she was leaving soon, and he would be staying here?

"This is much better than robe," he said, pulling on his shirt.

"It is amazing how cool I am, out here in this heat," I said, nodding.

"You do like technology?" he asked.

"Yes, I think it's great," I said. "They have some really fantastic things here. I can't wait to see what else they have down there."

"Look at the computer," he said.

I was confused. I didn't see his computer in his hand. He reached into a pocket on his pants and pulled out a small black thing. He pushed and pulled something, and the thing unfolded or expanded to become his computer. He laughed when he saw my eyes bugging out of my head.

"Wow! How did you do that?" I asked.

"Salmoony show me how," he explained. "I show you on yours."

"Oh, I left mine inside," I said. I began to move in the direction to go get it, but right then the men who were digging began to shout.

We looked to see what was all the commotion. They were maneuvering a large crate out of the hole, and before they even had it uncovered, they pulled the end off the crate to reveal what looked like a large box.

"Great, it's a box inside a crate," I said.

"It's not just a box," Anita said, suddenly beside me. "That is one of the glider carts. As soon as it has been charged by the sun, it will be able to move by remote and carry supplies from here to there."

"It look like box," Nadir said.

"Of course it looks like a box," Anita snapped. "What else would a cart look like?"

"I guess it just doesn't look like a cart because it doesn't have any wheels," I said. I took a few steps toward it to get a closer look as they pulled it out of the crate.

"Of course it has no wheels!" Anita shouted. "It is a glider cart, and glider carts do not have wheels!"

"Yes, of course," I agreed, hoping she would stop yelling at us.

"Let the ones who will be leaving get some sleep,"

Beezeeneck said loudly. "Our supplies are ready to go, and we just need to let the glider cart to charge up. The rest of you who are staying, Dr. Conrad-Bean is now in charge."

My dad and I went with the majority of the people back into the shelter. I was just about to tell him I wanted to take a shower when Beezeeneck made an announcement.

"Everyone, we need you to help transport supplies to the glider cart now. We want to get everything ready for tonight. Those who are leaving, you can get some rest if you like, or help us, and change into hiking boots when you awaken. We have plenty of hands for loading, if everyone else helps."

When we entered the lounge, I was surprised to see so many packages, large and small, stacked and ready to go. We each grabbed as much as we could carry and headed for the ladder. I wondered why they did not have a conveyor belt or melting elevator or some other fancy way to transport these items, but I gladly went along with what everyone else was doing. The packages were heavy and I thought about what great assistance the glider cart would be for those who were going on such a long journey. I secretly hoped they would send a helicopter or some other form of transportation back to get us so we would never have to make the long trek across the desert on foot.

We loaded the items into the glider cart and went back underground to get another load, which looked to be the final load. I was relieved, because I was tired, worn out, sleepy and I still wanted that shower.

As soon as we finished putting the last package into the glider cart, Wickersham, who had finally decided he could see the light of day and not die, grabbed a little device that was in a pocket on the front of the cart, which I soon discovered was the remote control.

"Let's see how this baby works!" he shouted, fiddling with the switches.

"Do you think we should try it before it is fully charged?" Dr. Conrad-Bean asked, in a tone that meant, 'we should not try it before it is fully charged.'

"It has plenty of time to become fully charged," Wickersham said, with an awful grin on his face. He was making me think that perhaps I should mention to my dad that we could leave with this expedition, because I didn't really want to spend any time with Wickersham in the shelter, even though the place was big enough that we could easily avoid each other.

Still, watching the glider cart was fascinating. Wickersham got it going, slowly at first, then a little faster.

"You need to stay with it," Dr. Conrad-Bean shouted at him, as a few of us began to jog along beside it, "to be able to control the altitude. You don't want it to crash into anything that might be sticking up."

"It has sensors," Wickersham shouted back, as he, too, began to run with it. "It can't crash into anything! It's impossible!"

At that moment, it shot ahead of us, at least a hundred meters, and we all picked up our pace in an attempt to catch it.

"Bring it back!" Dr. Conrad-Bean shouted from way behind us.

The glider cart abruptly stopped and parked itself in the sand. I was caught up in the crowd, and, although my legs were tired, I pushed myself to keep up with the others who were running after it. Nadir, Sammy, Salwa and Lena were the first ones to arrive, with my dad, Anita and Wickersham somewhat behind them. I was the last one to get there, breathing hard. I looked back at how far we had come, which was quite a distance. We were nearly out of the valley of the Four Quadrants; beyond the little memorial cemetery my dad had created After The Great Devastation. I could just barely see Dr. Conrad-Bean standing near the entrance to the shelter along with a bunch of the other people, maybe fifteen, who were watching us from a distance.

"Lena, why you are not sleeping?" Nadir asked. "You need rest for journey."

"I am not tired," she said rebelliously.

"Why did it stop?" my dad asked, turning to Wickersham.

"I have not a clue," Wickersham said, looking at the glider cart as if it were going to give him a clue.

"Probably not all charging," Nadir said. "You make it go too soon."

"Now you listen here, you little punk," Wickersham said, looking like he was about to punch Nadir in the nose.

"Shhh!" Sammy said, perking up.

"Don't you shush me," Wickersham said, then he stopped.

We all heard it, a faint whistling. Before I knew what was happening, my dad and Nadir pulled me to the ground near the glider cart, and they both fell across me. The sound grew louder very quickly, suddenly becoming a deafening roar, ending with the sound of a giant explosion, which shook the ground where we where huddled.

"My Lord Jesus," my dad said, right in my ear. I doubt that I would have been able to hear him if he were even a few inches away from me.

I could hear buzzing of voices as we scrambled to our feet. I glanced back and saw smoke coming from the exact spot where Dr. Conrad-Bean had been standing. My dad was pulling me, and Wickersham was fiddling with the control when Nadir took it from his hand. I saw Anita pulling Salwa, and I grabbed Lena, who was struggling to get to her feet. Sammy came up behind her, and we started moving out of the valley as quickly as we possibly could.

My ears were still ringing as we rushed down the path I had traveled a few days ago — or was it a few weeks ago? — that had led me to my dad. I kept feeling like I was going to fall, but someone else was always supporting me, and I think I was doing the same for others.

We were moving fast, and I became aware that the glider cart was moving along beside us. I looked longingly at it, wishing I could hitch a ride in it, but since that was not possible, I just kept moving my legs, one foot in front of the other, as fast as I could go.

I did not hear the warning whistle, but rather, I felt it, and I turned to my dad in terror. His eyes were sharp and ready. He quickly pulled me to the ground again, and I covered my ears and closed my eyes as I felt the others fall down around me. Again, a deafening sound, although not quite as loud as the first. I was not sure if it was because we were farther away from the site of impact, or because my ears were covered and still ringing, but the shaking of the ground did not seem as jolting as it had been the first time. We stayed huddled on the ground for a moment and were just beginning to move when I heard it again. I plugged my ears tightly and waited for the explosion, which came in just a few seconds, then the shaking, which was noticeably less intense than the first two times.

We stayed in that position for a few minutes, huddled together on the ground with the glider cart between us and the direction from which the explosions were coming. Slowly, we started moving, looking at each other for assurance. None of us had been injured, thankfully, but I did not want to think about the ones who were back at the shelter. We pulled ourselves and each other to our feet.

"We are getting close," Nadir said. I could barely hear him through the ringing of my ears.

"Close to what?" Anita asked, turning her head to the left and right dramatically. "I do not see a thing any where out here."

"We are getting close to our village," Nadir said nodding his head in a forward direction. "About one more hour of walking fast."

"It took us much longer to get to the valley," I said, trying to make sense of what he was saying.

"We are traveling very fast," Nadir explained.

"So, what's the good of your village?" Anita asked.

"Yeah, did you not bring all the good stuff to the bomb shelter?" Wickersham asked, doing something with the remote control to the glider cart.

"We have much food there," Lena said.

"And we have shelter there," my dad added, giving Wickersham a hand. "Nadir, Sammy, come and hold this, and we might be able to get it going again."

The two men and two boys worked on the glider cart for a few minutes. I noticed I was very thirsty.

"Do we have any water in there?" I asked. What good would the supplies be, if we had not brought any water?

"Just wait a few minutes, Layla," my dad said patiently.

Thinking about being thirsty was just making me more thirsty, so I tried to think about something else — but I could not allow myself to think about the obvious, the awful, the unthinkable, the fate of the people we had just left back at the underground shelter.

"I wish to bring computer," Lena said, "to contact *Baba* to let him know I not get hurt."

"I have my computer," Nadir said, stepping away from the glider cart and reaching for his pocket.

"Don't use it!" my dad shouted.

Nadir and Lena froze and looked at my dad with confusion.

"Why I not call my father?" Lena asked.

"The missiles," my dad said. "Once we let down the shield, they, whoever they are, the enemy, was able to locate us by our transmissions. We must not use the computer until we know we are in a safe place. Does anyone else have a computer with them?"

"I don't," I said, shaking my head.

"Nope, me neither," Wickersham said. "And I know exactly where I left it."

"And it is probably blown to smithereens by now," Anita said, putting it in nice, graphic terms for us.

"It's inside the bomb shelter, you dodo," Wickersham said to her, as he pulled on some kind of wire on the glider cart.

"And the bomb shelter is only bomb-proof when it is sealed," Anita replied, "which it was not, when we left."

"I almost cannot believe it," Wickersham said, stepping back from the glider cart.

"What? What is it?" my dad asked, looking for an answer on the glider cart.

"I stay underground, sealed up, for more than nine years, safe on the inside," Wickersham said, rubbing his head from front to back, "and the day I step out for the first time, the shelter is bombed and its safety is no longer."

Salwa began to cry. "*Baba*," she said softly. Lena put her arm around Salwa's shoulder.

I felt like crying, too. My dad was right here, with me, but Lena, Salwa, Nadir and Sammy had most likely just lost their fathers. They, too, had been safe in the village all this time, until today's tragedy. Suddenly, I felt responsible, because, as Nadir had said earlier, life had remained the same for years until I arrived and changed everything, both for the people of my dad's village, and also those who had been living inside the shelter. It was possible that twenty-two people had just died because of me.

"I think it will go now," my dad said, as he finished whatever he was doing to the glider cart.

Wickersham used the remote control and the glider

cart began to move. We moved along with it, picking up our pace so we could get to the village in a hurry.

We heard no more missiles, no more explosions, and eventually my hearing returned to something close to normal as we approached the little group of huts.

"We fix some food," Lena said, heading for the hut where we had eaten our meals, such a long time ago. Salwa followed her. I looked at my dad, and he nodded. I felt as if I should help them, too. I entered the tent and offered my assistance.

Working together, we were able to fix a meal their way within just a few minutes. My dad, Anita and Nadir had come into the hut to wait, while Wickersham and Sammy were doing something either outside or in another hut. My dad called to them to come and eat.

I did not have much of an appetite, but the others ate heartily. My stomach was tied in knots as I reflected on all those people whose lives had ended today. We did not converse beyond the remarks about how good the food was and questions from Anita and Wickersham as to what some of the foods were.

"Are you feeling okay?" my dad asked gently.

"Not really," I confessed. "It was all my fault." I could not stop the tears. I broke down and cried in front of everyone.

"Do not blame yourself," Nadir said. He handed me a cloth so I could blow my nose.

"Yeah, you did not shoot off those missiles," Wickersham said, chomping away at his food. "You had nothing to do with it."

"Yeah, but if I didn't have the idea to go and find clothes, we would not have found the entrance to the shelter and then they would not have put down the shield and then sent the transmissions that gave away the location," I cried.

"You had no idea about what was going to happen," my dad said, placing his hand on my shoulder. "You had a good idea, but circumstances caused the tragedy."

"I set the whole thing in motion," I said, while sobbing and wiping my nose and trying to catch my breath. "None of this would have happened if I had never even come here!"

"I am so thankful you came here," my dad said, hugging me close to him. "You have given me back my life again."

"Yeah, and I took away the lives of twenty-two other people!" I cried.

"We do not know they all have died," Nadir said.

"We can be pretty sure that most of them died," I said.

"Layla, everything happens for a reason," my dad said. "You must not take the blame for the evil deeds of another person."

"Who has done this?" Salwa asked. I realized she was also crying, but for another reason. "Who is the evil person?"

"That is what I intend to discover," Nadir said.

"That is what you intend to discover? Whatever you do, young fella, do NOT use your computer!" Wickersham said. "I hope you have it turned off."

Nadir reached into his pocket and pulled out the little folded up device that was his computer.

"Is this far enough off for you?" he asked, handing

it to Wickersham.

Wickersham took it from him and examined it. He handed it back to Nadir.

"I can't tell you for sure, but it looks to me to be all the way off." He took a big bite of some meat and chewed it loudly.

Lena stood up and took her plate and cup over to the large bowl she used to wash dishes.

Nadir put the computer back into his pocket. "I will keep it with me for the time when we may be able to use it."

"How do we know the way to go, without using the computer?" I asked, recalling the map feature.

"I know the way," Nadir said. He handed his empty plate to Lena, and my dad did, too.

"You know the way?" Wickersham said with a guffaw. "You know the way?"

"Do you just repeat things and make them sound ridiculous?" I said, fed up with Wickersham's disrespect of Nadir.

"Do you just repeat things and make them sound ridiculous?" Wickersham asked, mimicking my voice.

"Wickersham, please," my dad said. "Like it or not, we are in this together. We need to get along, and we need to show respect, even for these five young people we have; especially for these five young people. They are our future, and we need to take care of them, for they will soon be taking care of us."

"They will soon be taking care of us?" Wickersham hooted. "That will be the day, when they are taking care of us!"

"I agree with Obiad," Anita said.

"Of course you agree with Obiad," Wickersham said in a patronizing voice. "You have been all over him since the second he arrived at the shelter."

"I have not!" she said. She raised her hand as if she were going to slap Wickersham, but she stopped, withdrew her hand and took a deep breath.

"We are the adults here," my dad reminded them. "Let us set a fine example for the young ones."

"Excuse me, sir, but I am nineteen years old," Nadir told my dad.

My dad smiled at him. "Yes, you are. And we are at least twice your age."

"Yes, sir," Nadir said respectfully.

"So, what's the plan, Maloof?" Wickersham asked, snatching a piece of bread off my plate. Everyone else was finished eating, and Lena was collecting the rest of the plates. I had only been able to take two bites, but I did finish my water.

"You are letting Obiad be the leader?" Anita asked incredulously. "You rascal!"

Wickersham turned to face her. "Shut it, Anita," he said. "I did not want to leave the safety of the shelter in the first place, but here I am, with you turkeys, so I have to make the best of it. I wanna know, what is the plan, Maloof?"

"I must ask that you show respect to each of us," my dad said, "if you plan to stay with us."

"So, are you going to stay here, in these shacks?" Wickersham asked, waving his hand in the air.

"What do you want to do?" my dad asked. "You

have the right to make your own decision about your future."

"I cannot make my own decision, because I am stuck here with you!" Wickersham shouted, leaning into my dad's face.

"You should be glad you are here with us and not back with the others, because you would be dead!" I shouted. I had to scoot back, because I had suddenly stood up and leaned into Wickersham's face without even being aware of it. I sat on the stool and tried to breathe normally.

"Layla, you have no reason to lose your temper," my dad said calmly, covering my hand with his on the table.

"I'm sorry, Daddy, but he's just so—" I saw the look on my dad's face and knew when to stop talking. "I am sorry."

"So, Maloof, you are in charge," Wickersham said, shaking his finger at my dad. "I am no leader. I am not going to take responsibility for this sorry lot. So, what are we going to do?"

"We have to go on," my dad said. "We started the journey, and we need to finish it, no matter what the consequences."

"What if the place we are going," Anita asked, throwing her hands up in the air, "what if they are the ones who sent the bombs today?"

"We have to take that chance," my dad said, shrugging his shoulders.

"Why do we have to take that chance?" Wickersham said, now mimicking my dad's voice.

"What alternative do we have?" my dad asked. "We

can't go back to the bomb shelter. We can't stay here. We must move on." He pointed to three places on the table as he spoke, back, center and forward.

"Why we cannot stay here?" Sammy asked. He had been so quiet, I had almost forgotten he was with us.

"Son, we have lived here for nine years," my dad said, turning to face him. "We were not aware of the other people who had lived through the bombings. We have been able to survive, to exist, but we need to advance. We need to move on. Now that we know there are others, a city of at least a thousand people, we need to go there."

"What if they try to kill us?" Anita asked. She actually seemed excited by the prospect, a potential actress who wanted to stir things up and make life more dramatic than it really was, as if we had not already been through enough drama for one day.

"What if they don't?" I challenged her, narrowing my eyes at her.

My dad smiled.

"I know the way," Nadir again said. "I know where we go."

"And how would YOU know where we are to go?" Wickersham asked snidely. "I don't even know where we are going."

"I look at map on computer with Mr. Salmoony," Nadir said. "I know the way to get there."

"You look at map on computer?" Wickersham asked. "Salmoony doesn't know what he is looking for. Look at where all his intelligence got him! Dead!"

"Wickersham, give him a break!" my dad insisted.

"The boy is very intelligent."

"We do not know for sure that Salmoony is dead," Anita said quickly.

"Excuse me, please, sir, I see from where transmissions come and I know the area. I live in this area all my life and I know where and how to go there," Nadir said softly.

Finally Nadir had said something that Wickersham could not argue with. The two of them looked at each other, and for a minute, I thought Wickersham was going to break down or something.

"Wickersham, you are welcome to stay here," my dad said, "and anyone else who thinks this is the best place to be. As for me and my daughter, we are going to this place that Nadir knows, the place where we have hope for a future."

"I shall go with you," Lena stated.

"I go with you," Salwa added.

"Well, I certainly am not going to stay here, in this God-forsaken place," Anita announced, "especially if you are not going to be here." I thought she was going to stick out her tongue at Wickersham, but she restrained herself at the last second.

"I beg your pardon," my dad said quietly, "but this place has been anything but God-forsaken. This place has been a blessing, and God has given us life here."

"Amen!" I agreed.

"I am going with you," Anita clarified, with a look of anger on her face. I was hoping she would decide to stay right here, with Wickersham, so they would not make trouble for us on the journey.

"And I go with you," Sammy said.

Salwa smiled shyly at him and I thought I saw something special between them.

"Best for us to sleep now and begin to walk after sun go down," Nadir suggested.

"Layla, you and the girls, and Anita, you go to our hut and sleep there. We boys will sleep in Nadir's hut," my dad said.

I stood up and began to head for the flap in the tent, with Lena and Salwa close behind me.

"Are you telling me what to do?" Wickersham asked, his anger again beginning to rise.

"I am not telling you anything," my dad said, getting up from the table, "unless you plan to go with us. If you do, I must ask that you follow my directions."

"I will think about it," Wickersham said. "I might just go back and see who is still alive back there."

"Be my guest," my dad said, leaving the hut. "We will be heading out this evening, take it or leave it," he called as he stepped outside.

Lena, Salwa and I went to my dad's hut and got comfortable on the bedrolls. I did not know what Anita was doing, but I was really sleepy and more than a little upset that I had not been able to take another shower before we left. I closed my eyes and let my tired body relax as I drifted into a dreamless sleep.

CHAPTER 8

When I awakened, the hut was dark inside. I took a moment to realize where I was and why I was there. For a few seconds, I had a feeling of gloom and doom, and could not recall why; then I remembered the horrible incident earlier in the day. I heard hushed voices whispering and I recognized the voices of Lena and Salwa, but I could not understand what they were saying.

"Can you please cut out the foreign chatter?" Anita said, with an irritation in her voice. I was hoping our journey would be swift and that we would be exhausted each time we stopped, so she would not have the energy to pick on us, or even talk to us.

"Layla!" my dad called from outside the hut. "Are you about ready to go?"

"Yes, Daddy," I called. I quickly straightened up the blanket and went out of the hut, with Lena, Salwa and Anita close behind me.

"I hope you are well rested," my dad said. He was putting some additional items in the glider cart.

"As well rested as I can be," I replied. I felt as if I could sleep for a couple more days, but right now, we did not have that luxury. I would have to wait until we arrived at our destination before I would be able to really get another good night's sleep — mainly because we would be travelling during the night and sleeping during the day.

"Alright, alright," Wickersham growled, as he emerged from one of the huts. "I will go with you, but only to make sure these young people don't get into any trouble."

"And I will be keeping my eye on YOU, to be sure YOU don't get into any trouble!" Anita scowled at him.

"Okay, Wickersham, do you have the remote control for the glider cart?" my dad asked.

"Of course I have it," Wickersham wailed, checking his pocket. He then ducked back into the hut and reappeared a moment later with the remote control in his hand.

"Let us ask God's blessing before we start on our journey," my dad said. "Eternal God, look upon us as we make our way to a place yet unknown to us. We ask for travelling mercies, every step of the way. We ask that You go before us and make a way for us. Give us favor with the people we will meet, on the way and when we arrive at our destination. In the mighty name of Jesus we pray. Amen."

"Amen," the rest of us said.

"Okay, Mr. Nadir, do you want to lead the way?" my dad asked.

Nadir began walking away from the little cluster of huts in a direction I had not yet gone. My dad got in step beside Nadir. The rest of us followed them, with Wickersham controlling the glider cart.

The pace was much faster than what was comfortable for me, so I trotted along behind my dad without talking. I heard snippets of the conversation between Nadir and my dad, but I was using all my energy to keep up with them, so did not say anything for a long time. The night was beginning to get dark, and the stars were coming out in droves. The moon rose behind us, giving us a nice light by which to travel. The landscape looked all white and smooth, in every direction, as far as the eye could see. We kept following Nadir on an unseen trail, and he was quite confident in knowing which way to go.

We walked all night, our pace slowing after a couple of hours. When the moon was directly overhead, I could see just a few shrubs in the distance, but all around us, there was nothing but sand.

"I hope we don't come across any snakes out here," Anita announced loudly. She had been trying to catch up with my dad all night, but she was just huffing and puffing along a few paces behind me.

"We may see some in the early morning," Nadir called back to her. "They like to come out just before the sun comes up."

"Oh no!" she shrieked.

I laughed, hoping Nadir had said that just to bug her. I was not a big fan of snakes either, although I could not ever remember seeing a real one.

We came upon a big pile of rocks, and my dad suggested we take a break and have some water and a snack. Lena and Salwa were ready to jump into action to make the snack, but my dad already had something prepared that he had brought from the underground shelter. I sat on a large boulder beside my dad and ate some kind of dried meat and a few nuts, and washed them down with some water.

"How many days do you think it will take for us to get there?" Anita asked Nadir, with her mouth full of food.

"Don't you mean, how many nights will it take for us to get there?" Wickersham asked her. "During the day, we won't be doing much moving."

"Okay, if you want to put it that way, how many nights do you think it will take for us to get there?" she asked.

"Maybe ten nights of walking, maybe more," Nadir said. He took a drink of his water.

"Do we have enough water?" I asked. I had seen some water bottles, but we had to keep eight people hydrated as we crossed the desert.

"We have the camel pouches," Wickersham said. He must have seen the question mark expression on my face. "Pouches we wear on our backs that are filled with water."

"We will come to the natural springs and we refill there," Nadir said.

"Natural springs?" I asked. That sounded very inviting.

"Yes, perhaps we will arrive tomorrow night."

"I cannot wait to dive in there!" Anita said. "That will be so delicious, don't you agree?"

"Miss Anita, it is for drinking water, not for swimming water," Nadir said politely, as he replaced the lid on his water bottle.

"Look, kid, you cannot tell me where I can swim and where I cannot swim," Anita told him.

"Anita, let us get our water first and you can swim later," my dad suggested.

"Obiad, you have ALL the good ideas," she said, leaning close to him. Her over-dramatization was making me feel a bit ill. I expected her to start petting him.

"We must be on the way," Nadir said, gathering up his things and putting them into his pack.

"Can we just take a little nap?" Wickersham asked. He was lying on his back on a huge rock.

"This is not the place to take a nap," Nadir said. "You do know, snakes live in rocks?"

Anita jumped so high, I thought she was going to latch onto the moon. "Come on, guys, what are we waiting for? Let's get going!" she shouted.

We collected everything we had brought and put it all back into the glider cart. Wickersham slowly got up from his rock bed and joined us, putting the glider cart into motion.

The rest of the night was uneventful until just as the sun was coming up. Salwa cried out suddenly, and we came to a halt.

"Salwa, what is it?" Nadir asked, running back to where she and Sammy were bringing up the rear.

"My foot!" she yelled, falling to the ground. She grabbed her ankle and began rocking back and forth.

"Has she broken her ankle?" Anita asked, almost hopefully.

My dad sat on the ground and examined it. "I think it may be sprained, but it is not broken," he said, looking up to the rest of us as we leaned over her.

"I cannot walk," Salwa cried. "Please, do not leave me alone."

"I will stay with you," Sammy offered, squatting down beside her. "Leave us with some food and water. Come get us after you find the city."

"We are not leaving anyone here," my dad said.

"We are going to help you."

"She is going to throw a wrench in the whole operation," Wickersham complained. "We'll never get there with Miss Lame holding us back."

"Just a short distance to good place to stop and make camp," Nadir said. "We help Salwa walk."

"Can we put her in the glider cart?" I asked. She was little, she was light. I thought it might work.

"That is a splendid idea!" my dad said.

"We have no room for her inside the glider cart," Wickersham said. He seemed to be disgusted with the idea of helping someone.

"We can take out some of the stuff and carry it," I said. "Then there will be room for her."

"Yes, you have good idea," Nadir agreed.

Wickersham reluctantly let us remove some of the items from the glider cart and Nadir and my dad lifted Salwa into the cart. Anita found a first aid kit with some kind of cold pack and Sammy reached in the cart in order to wrap it around Salwa's swollen ankle. When we started walking again, Sammy stayed beside the glider cart so he could encourage Salwa. Lena made her way to the front of the pack, to walk by Nadir. I walked beside my dad, with Anita tagging along on the other side of him. She kept trying to start a conversation with him, but he obviously wasn't interested, because he didn't reply. I was so tired, I could not have spoken, even if I had had anything to say.

"Just up ahead," Nadir announced. "A few trees where we set up camp."

I looked up to see the few trees. My energy was

renewed; I had only seen a couple of live trees since The Great Devastation! I was able to walk quickly to them, which were much farther from us than they had looked when Nadir had first mentioned them. I nearly raced to them and had to restrain myself from giving them each a hug. The last time I had hugged a tree, I had gotten a bunch of pokey things on me. Up close, trees are not all smooth and huggable. They are rough and have all these little sticks coming off of them.

The sun was now rising and the temperature along with it. I was grateful to those who quickly erected the two tents, and as soon as they were ready, I dove into the one my dad had designated for the females.

"Layla, don't you want to eat before you sleep?" my dad asked, peeking his head in the tent flap.

"I am too tired to eat," I said, ready to doze off. I spread out a blanket and was about to make it my bed when I heard some commotion outside the tent. I had nearly forgotten about poor Salwa, whom Nadir and Sammy carried into the tent.

"You can put her right here," I said, offering the bed I had just prepared.

"Thank you, Layla," Salwa said. She had such a pained expression on her face, I was ashamed of thinking only of myself.

"Do you want me to bring you something to eat?" I offered, as Nadir and Sammy left our tent.

"No, thank you," Salwa said. "I want to sleep and forget about this pain."

I left the tent to find Anita.

"Do we have anything we can give Salwa for the pain?" I asked her.

"I believe we have pain relievers in the first aid kit," she answered.

"No, no pill for Salwa," Sammy said. "She need natural."

"Natural?" I asked. "What do you mean?"

Nadir appeared with some kind of leaves in his hand. "Let her to chew on these. She feel relief from pain."

"Are you sure that is safe?" I asked.

"We do it many times," Nadir said, exchanging glances with Sammy.

"Okay," I said, taking the leaves from Nadir. I tried to get some meaning from his eyes, but he would not share the secret with me.

I went into the tent where Lena was singing softly to Salwa in Arabic. When Salwa saw the leaves in my hand, she smiled and thanked me. I gave them to her and she began to chew on them. I could see the relaxation on her face and she soon fell asleep. Lena and I made our beds and in a few minutes, I was also asleep.

CHAPTER 9

A strange sound awakened me. This time, I knew exactly where I was, and I was afraid something bad had happened to Salwa. I sat up and looked at her, but she, Lena and Anita were sound asleep. The day was still bright, so I figured we still had some time to sleep before the cool of the evening would allow us to continue on our trek.

I leaned back on the blanket, trying to make the sandy ground beneath feel more comfortable, and I heard the sound again. It was not like a whistle, but it was a shrill sound, or a whining sound. The other three were still sleeping; they obviously had not heard anything. I poked my head out of the tent to see if I could find out what was making the sound. I was not ready to go out there, in case it might be something dangerous, like a wild animal. At first, I did not see anything. Out of the corner of my eye, I saw some movement, and I nearly jumped out of my skin until I realized it was only Nadir. He was crouched down beneath one of the trees, looking to his left and to his right. Something near him moved, and he jumped at it.

I heard the sound again. It seemed to be closer to us now. I stepped out of the tent and Nadir immediately turned to me.

"Shhh!" he said quietly.

"What is it?" I whispered. "What is that sound?"

Then I saw what he had in his hand, what he had caught: it was a little rabbit, brown and white. I had seen one before, but not like this, not so close. As I stepped closer to Nadir, I saw that he had another one, trapped inside a type of a net.

"Are we going to eat those?" I asked, wincing. I knew we were meat eaters, but I could not imagine eating those furry, cute little things.

"Did you hear the howling?" Nadir whispered, motioning for me to squat down beside him.

"I heard something," I whispered back, lowering myself to his level. "I didn't know what it was."

We heard it again, louder, closer. I looked at Nadir with an expression that must have revealed my fear; I had no idea what might be howling, but I did not want it or them to be coming near us.

"We hear the wolves," Nadir said, his voice very low. "When wolves come from mountains to here, they look for food. Wolves are very hungry when hunting during daytime."

"Can we leave some food for them and get out of here?" I asked, looking toward where I thought the sound of the howling had come from.

"I will take the rabbits far away from us so wolves go there and not come here, to follow us," Nadir explained.

"I'll go with you," I said.

"No, you stay with group. I go to south. I lead wolves off trail. When sun is down, you and all the people go to west. Go straight to west and I find you."

"Straight to the west? How will I know, in the dark, which way is west?"

"Sun will be exactly ahead when goes down. Mark direction and follow, to west." He pointed toward the west. "When you see North Star, keep on your right. North Star stay to your right side."

I nodded. I preferred to not go on a hunt to distract wolves. What Nadir was saying was perfectly logical; however, I had no idea how to find the North Star. I figured I would tell my dad, and he would know. My dad knew everything.

Nadir vanished, going to the south. I decided to try to get some more sleep so I would have enough energy to walk all night. I wondered how Salwa was feeling, but when I went back into the tent, she was still asleep. I heard the howling of the wolves again, and a chill went down my back. I said a quick prayer for Nadir, to be safe on his mission.

I could not sleep. I was just lying there, thinking about Nadir, thinking about Salwa's injury, thinking about Anita trying to latch on to my dad, thinking about this journey. The thought popped into my head that the first boy who had ever kissed me was now dead, and, no matter what my dad and the others said to me, it was my fault. Poor little Essom was also dead, and he was just a little kid.

Then it occurred to me that perhaps they had not all died. Perhaps Jamal and Essom and some of the others had not been killed by the missile attack. Yes, they could have been deep inside the shelter, saved from the explosion. It was too painful to think that they were all dead because of me; some of them did survive, I was sure of it.

I think I was going in and out of sleep, but I felt as if I were not sleeping at all. I heard my dad's voice arousing the troops and I realized I had not heard the howling in quite some time. I rolled up my blanket and climbed out of the tent so I could tell my dad where Nadir had gone.

Suddenly I was frozen by fear. What if the wolves had stopped howling because they had caught Nadir? What if they were tearing him limb from limb?

No, I could not allow those negative thoughts to bombard my consciousness! Nadir was an experienced hunter and he knew what he was doing.

"Daddy!" I called, when I saw him looking into the distance. The sun had gone down so it was getting hard to see anything in the distance.

"Not now, Layla," my dad said. His forehead was all wrinkled and he seemed to be very upset. "We have no idea what happened to Nadir. Without him to guide us, we do not know the direction to take. We need to keep moving, but he seems to have vanished!"

"I know where he is," I said, trying to sooth my dad's worrying.

"You do?" my dad said. He stopped his scanning of the landscape and looked at me. "Where did he go?"

"We heard some wolves howling so he took some little rabbits to lead them off our trail," I said.

"What kind of a plan is that?" Wickersham said, joining us. "They eat the rabbits, then they just follow the boy's scent back to us and they eat us up! We are sitting ducks, just waiting here for them to come and eat us."

"No, he knows what he is doing," I said. "He went to the south, to get the wolves away from us, and he wants us to go to the west, straight west, and he will catch up with us. We should get going as soon as we can."

"Now we are taking orders from a little girl?" Wickersham sneered. He spit in the other direction, but it felt personal to me. His gross action made my stomach turn. "And how do we know which way is west when it is pitch dark outside? We have no way to follow the sun."

"The sun just went down right over there," I said, pointing.

"Do you have any idea, little girl, how hard it is to keep your sense of direction when you are walking in the dark?" Wickersham asked me, leaning into my personal space.

I took a step away from him and his stinky breath.

"Come on, Wickersham, how do you think anyone has ever navigated at night?" my dad asked.

By this time, Anita was coming over to join us while Lena and Sammy were packing up the tents. Salwa was sitting on a bundle of blankets with her foot slightly elevated.

"Well, don't you know, they used computers and navigational systems," Wickersham said to my dad. Wickersham seemed to be in attack mode towards anyone who spoke to him.

"No, before computers, how did they navigate at night?" my dad asked, trying to get him to think.

"I guess they just stayed home, back in their caves," Wickersham said, crossing his arms in defiance of my dad.

"I think you came out of your cave a little too soon," my dad said, shaking his head slowly.

Anita started laughing as if my dad had just told the funniest joke in the world. She was really exaggerating it, and the high pitches in her squealing were really bothering me.

"Obiad, you are SOOOO funny!" Anita said. "Out of his cave too soon, that is a good one!"

"My point is," my dad said, ignoring her, "we can navigate by using the North Star as a point of reference."

"Yes!" I shouted. "That is what Nadir said for us to do!"

"Well, I can tell you one thing," Wickersham said, as if he had not already told us enough, "I do not plan to take orders from a kid, any kid, no matter what you say."

My dad stepped over so he was standing directly in front of Wickersham, facing him. My dad was a little bit taller than Wickersham, so he looked down into his face.

"I will tell you one thing," my dad said, using a very calm voice, "if you don't want to follow us on the path we are taking, you can gather up your things and either go back to wherever you want to go, or you can stay right here, for all I care. We cannot function as a group with one person constantly challenging our every move. Just give me the remote control for the glider cart so we can take our supplies with us." My dad turned away from Wickersham and faced the rest of us. "Come on, let's get moving! We are going west!"

Anita gave Wickersham a very childish look before turning away from him. We quickly gathered our things and Sammy and my dad lifted Salwa into the glider cart.

"With one man down, you are going to need me," Wickersham grumbled. "Go ahead, Maloof, I'm on your side."

My dad did not answer him, but just started to lead us toward the west. After a very short time, I could understand Wickersham's point of view, because I could not tell if we were still going west. I did not say anything, assuming my dad knew the direction we were to go.

Sammy and Lena stayed by the glider cart so they could converse with Salwa as we traveled. I walked a short distance behind my dad and Anita, who had claimed her spot beside him and was talking his ear off. Wickersham brought up the rear, controlling the glider cart and mumbling to himself.

I kept looking to my left to see if Nadir were on his way. After walking for a couple of hours, we still had not heard nor seen him. My dad called for us to take a short break, and Lena quickly whipped up a snack of hummus and bread for us. The food she prepared was always so delicious, I made a mental note to ask her to teach me some of her cooking tricks once we reached our destination.

I kept hoping Nadir would catch us while we were stopped, but he didn't come. When it was time to start walking again, I looked in vain for him, straining to see him in the darkness to the south. I did not know if he had a lantern or flashlight with him, but we were carrying and wearing all kinds of lights, so he would be able to see us easily from a distance.

"So, how far is it to these natural springs?" Anita asked loudly. "The boy said we would be getting to them tonight. I cannot WAIT to get into that fresh, clear water."

"I have no idea," my dad said. "I have not walked this far before. I am just following Nadir's directions."

I wanted to ask my dad which star was the North Star, but I did not get an opportunity to speak to him privately. I kept looking to the sky on my right, and I could see lots of bright stars in that direction. Maybe the North Star was the one that was the brightest? I was just so thankful that my dad knew which direction to lead us.

The evening was quite warm, as had been each evening since I arrived on this side of the world, but I became aware that my skin was beginning to feel clammy. The air seemed sort of muggy, and I glanced up to be sure that brightest star was still in place. I sort of panicked when I could not see even one single star in the sky.

"Daddy!" I called.

My dad stopped and turned to look at me. Anita kept walking and talking to him, unaware that he was no longer beside her.

"Daddy, I can't see any stars any more," I said. "I mean, I can't see the North Star any more."

"Yes, we have come under a cloud cover, but we will be fine," my dad said reassuringly.

Up ahead of us, Anita finally stopped talking and she noticed that we had all stopped walking.

"What's going on back there?" she shouted. Even in the darkness, I was sure that she stamped her foot on the sand, like a little kid who was frustrated.

"Nothing, we are coming," my dad called to her, as we started again.

"Daddy, are those trees up ahead?" I asked, looking past him at some odd shapes.

He turned a bright flashlight so he could see farther ahead of him.

"Yep, it looks like we are coming to a forest of

some sort," he said, shining the light back and forth to illuminate what looked like hundreds of trees.

"A forest!" I said with excitement. "I have always wanted to see a forest!"

"Oh, that is just great," Wickersham complained, as we approached the trees, which looked to be quite dense. "Not only will we have to make a path through the forest, we will have to make a path wide enough to fit the glider cart. This is never going to work."

"Wickersham, you dummy," Anita said. "You can just raise it to hover above the trees."

"I know that," he said, as if he had already known that. "But what about the girl? We can't have her hovering above the trees."

We stopped at the edge of the forest. Wickersham had made a good point. It was one thing for all our supplies to be flying over our heads and over the trees, but what about Salwa? It might be scary for her, and even dangerous. If the glider cart were to tip, she could fall out and get hurt even worse than she already was; and it would again be my fault, because it was my idea for her to ride in it.

"I carry Salwa on my back," Sammy offered.

"We can make a carrier from sticks and a blanket, and we can take turns carrying her, two of us at a time," my dad suggested.

"No, best way is like this," Sammy said. He took a blanket and rolled it up. He lifted Salwa out of the glider cart and set her on the ground. "Stand on good foot," he instructed, as he somehow wrapped the blanket through her legs and over her shoulders. He did it so quickly, then he turned around, grabbed the loose ends of the blanket, squatted in front of her, stood up and pulled the ends of the blanket around his waist. Now Salwa was like a backpack on Sammy's back.

"How did you do that?" Wickersham asked, clearly impressed.

"She not heavy," Sammy said. "Come, let us go."

We got into single file with my dad in the lead. Wickersham made the glider cart go high, above the trees, as we followed my dad through the dark and creepy forest. I could feel thousands of eyes on us, watching us from every direction, and I could hear unusual sounds: creakings and poppings and whistlings and cooings. None of the others seemed to be spooked, so I acted as if I were as brave as they were.

"I think we are going up a slight incline," my dad called back to the rest of us.

No one answered him, but I think it was because we all agreed, and it was getting difficult to talk while we walked. Our pace slowed considerably as we wove between the trees. Occasionally, my dad had to stomp down a path among the shrubbery and bushes.

"I just hope we get to those natural springs pretty soon," Anita announced. She was breathing very hard, and I was relieved to know that I was not the only one who was out of shape for this type of climb. My dad had put it mildly when he used the term 'slight incline.' Now it was more of a 'steep hill.' It was probably to our advantage to be climbing in the dark so we could not actually see how big the hill was that we were ascending.

As quickly as we entered the forest, we were out of it, on the other side. My dad turned to us as soon as we were all out in the open.

"It looks like we have a bit of a mountain to climb," he said, shining his bright flashlight ahead of us. The ground ahead changed from forest land to a rocky surface, but it did not seem to be impossible to cover.

We followed my dad for a few minutes and he stopped again. "It looks like we have a little bit of climbing to do," he said. "I certainly hope we are going in the right direction. I have not been able to see the North Star for quite some time, and I don't recall Nadir mentioning any hills we would need to cross. Well, here we go. I will do my best to pick out a path through these rocks. Let's have Salwa ride in the glider cart again. We can keep it close to us now."

"I can carry her still," Sammy said, but I could tell that he was relieved to get her off his back and put her back into the glider cart.

At first, we were walking over rocky ground. Soon the rocks became larger, and then we were climbing, hand over foot, using both hands to pull ourselves up onto the next boulder. My dad had to search for a way to go with the flashlight, then follow that way, since there was no path, and I was close behind him, paying attention to where he was putting each hand and foot. Looking above us, it seemed we had only a short distance to climb on rocks, but the actual climbing took a long time and was very difficult.

"Daddy, can you find a place where we can rest?" I called to him.

"I think I see a level surface just ahead," he called back to me.

Someone behind me screamed, and I heard the sickening sound of scraping, thumping, falling. I was in such a position so that I could not look back to see what had happened, or to whom.

"Are you all right?" I heard Sammy ask, as I pulled myself up to a little landing where my dad was waiting for me. I saw a small cave behind him and started to go toward it. I did not dare to look down to see the ones behind me, because, unknown to anyone else, I was afraid of heights. I knew I would get dizzy if I looked down and the bottoms of my feet would get tingly and, well, I could not allow myself to even think of what might happen.

"Stay away from the cave," my dad warned. "We have no idea of what may be inside it."

"Do you mean an animal, or something?" I asked, jumping back, suddenly more afraid of what was in front of me than the cliff behind me.

"We just don't know," my dad said.

"Did you hear someone scream down there?" I asked. "One of us, I mean?"

"No, did you?" He stood up and went over to the edge where we had climbed onto the landing.

"I think… someone might have fallen," I said slowly.

Even though he had a strong and bright flashlight, he was unable to see what had happened.

"I can't see the others," he said. "Is everything all right down there?" he called.

His voice echoed, "right down there?" and gave me a bit of a fright.

"We are coming up," Wickersham yelled. "Slight setback, ungh, ungh," he said. I assumed he was grunting as he was climbing, but I could not be sure.

"Do you need my help? (need my help?)" my dad asked.

"No, just keep shining the light so we can see the way," Wickersham answered.

"Daddy, I know we are in the desert in the middle of summer, but I am getting really cold," I said. I had been warm enough while I was climbing, but now that we were stopped, I was very cold. I pulled my legs up to my chest and hugged them.

"Send up the glider cart! (glider cart!)" my dad said to Wickersham. He turned to me and said, more quietly, "The high altitude, the air is thinner. We will be able to get a couple of blankets out of the cart."

"Coming up," Lena's tired voice said, and my dad moved back from the edge of the landing and helped pull her up. She was breathing very hard and her teeth were chattering. I held out my arms to her and she rushed over to me. We hugged each other, both to keep warm and because we were grateful to have made it this far.

"I heard a scream," I said, when her breathing had slowed to a near normal pace. "Is everyone okay? It sounded like someone was falling."

The glider cart arrived and my dad guided it back near the opening of the cave. He quickly pulled Salwa out and set her on the ground beside us, then he got blankets for us. We three huddled together with the blankets wrapped around us.

Salwa began sobbing softly. Lena and I hugged her to comfort her.

"Does your ankle hurt?" I asked.

She shook her head and reached down to her ankle.

"She cry because Miss Anita fall," Lena said quietly.

"Oh, no!" I cried, looking from Salwa to Lena. Their faces looked strange in the flicker of the light from the lantern. "Is she hurt?"

"I see her blood," Salwa said, between her sobs. She was looking down, inside the blanket, nearly hiding her face.

"What happened?" I asked, my heart racing.

"She fall on rocks," Salwa cried.

"Oh, no!" I repeated. "Is she…?" I could not finish my sentence, because even though she had been so annoying, I didn't want her to die.

"Coming through," Wickersham said loudly, so loudly I could tell he was right near the ledge.

We three girls leaned to see him hoist himself up with Anita on his back, strapped to him the same way Salwa had been strapped to Sammy earlier. The instant he made it to the ledge, he collapsed onto his stomach, with Anita, possibly unconscious, sprawled across him. He was panting hard, and at that very moment, Sammy appeared at the ledge and pulled himself up. He had to squeeze around Wickersham, but he was able to quickly scramble on all fours over to where we were sitting. My dad brought up the flashlight and began to examine Anita.

"Get… her… off… me," Wickersham said, one word with each breath.

Sammy moved quickly to him and with one movement he untied the blanket that had made Anita into a backpack. My dad gently rolled Anita off of Wickersham's back and began to examine her.

"She is alive," my dad said.

"Of course she is alive," Wickersham said, still trying to catch his breath. "Do you think I would have carried her up those rocks if she was dead? She is no light weight, you know."

My dad and Sammy checked Anita's eyes and the bones in her arms and legs.

"I don't think anything is broken," my dad said. "Did she hit her head when she fell?"

"I do not know if she hit her head," Sammy said.

"I saw her blood," Salwa said again.

"I can't see where she is bleeding," my dad said, looking for any signs of blood. "She seems to be breathing normally. Let us rest here for awhile and we can have a little snack. You girls might want to take a nap."

I realized that I was able to see everyone more clearly; daylight was beginning to come. I wondered if we would need to stay here all day, or if we would be able to continue. I was quite cold, so maybe on this hill or mountain the daytime temperatures would not be as high as they were down on the desert floor. I would much prefer to climb a mountain during the day instead of in the dark, if I had a choice. On the other hand, I was feeling weak and hungry, I could easily sleep all day, and I was hoping Nadir would catch up with us soon.

Wickersham pulled himself to his feet and got food and water out of the glider cart. He gave some to Salwa, Lena and me, then he joined Sammy and my dad to check on Anita. She seemed to be coming around, regaining consciousness, and she moved her head slowly to the left and right. I thought she was trying to speak, but it was hard to tell. I opened my packet of food to find some kind of nuts packed in some kind of cereal which was, surprisingly, very tasty. I gobbled it up in a few seconds, I think, and after I took a sip of water, I put my head between my raised knees so I could take a little nap in this sitting position. I was too cold to stretch out, even with a blanket.

Just as I was dozing off, my dad awakened me by touching me gently on the shoulder. I saw flashes of bright, white light behind my eyelids as I returned to this life.

"We need to keep Anita warm," he said. "Let's put down a blanket for her to lie on, and you three girls snuggle up as close to her as you can get. I'll put a couple more blankets on top of you."

"Maloof, use these thermal blankets," Wickersham instructed, pulling some other blankets out of the glider cart. "They radiate heat and they will keep the girls a lot warmer. I wish I would have thought to bring the thermal uniforms, but I had no idea we would be in temperatures this cold. How could I know we were going to climb some mountain?"

"Thermal blankets, good idea, Wickersham," my dad said, tucking the thermal blankets over and around us after I got on one side of Anita and Lena and Salwa got on the other side of her. The heat from the blankets felt so good, so soothing, so relaxing

Just as I was about to return to my target state of sleep, the strangest sound pulled me back once again to this reality, this time causing flashes of colorful light behind my eyelids. I felt a rumbling beneath me and the rocks were shaking. As I opened my eyes, I saw a touch of terror in Lena's eyes and I turned to see where she was looking, at the cave entrance beside us. Something was coming out of the cave!

CHAPTER 10

The glider cart, which was not gliding, but had been switched off and was just sitting on the landing near the cave entrance, began to shake. Almost instantly, the cart was shoved away from the cave entrance. My dad, Sammy and Wickersham jumped out of the way so quickly, I was almost expecting them to jump off the ledge as the glider cart went sailing off the landing. Some kind of animal with long white hair, a beard and long, black, ringed horns sticking off his forehead, came charging out of the cave and galloped down the side of the mountain with ease. Four more of these animals immediately followed, the last one a smaller version of the others, with little stubby horns. This last one was moving more slowly than the big ones and he stopped and looked curiously at us. He seemed to smile as he inspected us before he quickly jumped down the rocks to gracefully join the others.

My heart was pounding: I was petrified! What were these animals? Had the bigger ones even noticed us? Would they come back and eat us?

"*Inuzuh,*" Lena said with a laugh. She settled back in her spot, seemingly not worried.

"What?" I asked, huddling back under the covers. Since I was nearest to the rock wall, perhaps the animals would not be able to see me when they came back up here. I looked to be sure my dad, Sammy and Wickersham were safe, and they seemed to be fine. Wickersham had the remote control for the glider cart, and it looked like he was trying to get it to come back up the hill. He was cursing under his breath, something about it being damaged. I decided to let him worry about it while I got some sleep. If the animals were going to come and get us, I didn't have the energy to stay awake and watch for them.

"Those silly mountain goats!" my dad remarked, wrapping himself into a blanket.

Oh, so they were goats? As I drifted to sleep, I wondered if we could possibly get some goat cheese from them.

I awakened to bright sunlight shining in my face. The heat from the sun felt good, but the air temperature was still quite cool. I lifted my head to check on the others.

Anita was sleeping. She had turned onto her side, facing me. Salwa was asleep, snuggled up close to Anita's back, and Lena was curled around Salwa. Wickersham had apparently retrieved the glider cart, which was slightly battered and parked beside him as he was lying on his back on and snoring loudly. My dad and Sammy were not asleep, but were sitting on the other side of the entrance to the cave, talking quietly. They were both wrapped in blankets.

Again, I worried that Nadir would not be able to find us. After all, we were pretty well hidden, surrounded by large boulders on the side of a hill. I carefully pulled one blanket around me, making sure I did not pull the other blankets off of Anita, Salwa and Lena, and I kind of crawled over to where my dad and Sammy were sitting.

"What are you doing?" I asked. "Shouldn't you be trying to get some sleep?"

"We need to have someone keep watch," my dad said.

"Watch for what?" I said. "What would be way up

here? Oh, besides goats."

"Anything that might be dangerous up here," my dad said, taking a drink of water.

"Out in wild, some sleep while others awake," Sammy said. "We do this for our safety."

I nodded my head. They knew better than I did about safety matters up on the side of a hill.

"How is Nadir ever going to find us?" I asked. "If we can't see the bottom of this hill, he won't be able to see us, way up here."

"I was just thinking about that," my dad said, looking into the distance. "He could easily be going up another part of this hill and not even see us at all." He looked to his left and right, up and down the hill.

"We have no way to give him signal," Sammy said, shaking his head. "He has computer, we have no computer."

"Signal!" I said, a little too loudly. "We can send him a signal!"

"How to send signal? We have no way," Sammy said.

"Not a signal by computer," I said, really getting excited. "We can light a fire and he will see the smoke! He will know where we are and he can follow the smoke to us, here."

"Starting a fire is a good idea. It might also be a good idea for us to stay here for a while," my dad said, pulling his blanket tightly around himself. "We can let Nadir catch up to us while Salwa and Anita get a chance to recover."

"What happened to Anita, anyway?" I asked.

"Salwa said she saw her blood. Was she bleeding?"

"I could not find any blood on her," my dad said. "I think she just got the wind knocked out of her. Apparently, she took quite a fall and she landed flat on her back."

"You want me to start fire?" Sammy asked. Before my dad could answer, Sammy began gathering small rocks.

"Make a circle of rocks," my dad said. "I think we have some fire-starters in with our supplies."

"They do not fall out of cart?" Sammy asked, as he hastily made a circle of rocks.

"Oh, we better check our supplies," my dad said. "We lost some things when the glider cart went over the edge."

I was not about to look over the edge to see any items we had lost. One thing I knew about my fear of heights, I could not allow myself to look down. Just the thought of us being on a little ledge high above the earth made me queasy.

My dad had not even had a chance to check the supplies by the time Sammy had a bunch of dried leaves and sticks inside the circle of rocks. He grabbed one rock and started banging it on another rock. Sparks jumped off the rocks where they hit together and very soon the leaves caught fire.

I moved closer to the fire. The cave was now behind me, but I was pretty sure it was empty by this time. The heat from the fire felt so good on my chilly face. Sammy slithered down off the landing, the same way we had come, and returned quickly with a handful of leaves, some dry and some green.

"Green leaves make most smoke," he explained, as he must have seen the question mark on my face.

"Good thinking, young man," my dad said, reaching over to pat Sammy on his back.

The fire was burning quite well and sending a nice, thick stream of smoke into the air. It seemed a little odd to me that the smoke went straight up for a distance, then it turned in almost a right angle so it was going directly toward the sun.

My dad saw me watching the smoke and he must have read my mind.

"I assume that is the height of this hill, and the wind is blowing across the top of it," he explained. "Now, why don't you go and get another nap? Let's hope Nadir will catch up to us by tonight, and we can start walking again tomorrow morning."

"He won't be able to see the smoke in the dark," I said, still staring at the smoke. It was making a very beautiful white, puffy design against the brilliant blue sky, moving, changing, while keeping its beauty.

"No, but he will be able to see it all day, and it will lead him right to us. The smoke and the fire should also keep the mountain goats and any other animals away from here."

"Those goats sort of scared me this morning," I admitted. I pulled the blanket around me so I could make my way back to where the other females were sleeping.

"Do you want something to eat?" Sammy asked.

I glanced back at him. He was leaning over the fire with something on a stick, roasting it.

"No, thank you," I said. I kind of felt like I had left my stomach a few hundred feet below us, down on the level of the forest. "I'll have something later."

"I will have some of whatever you are cooking," Wickersham said, suddenly in a sitting position. "That is smelling pretty good!"

He went over to the other men while I stretched out beside Anita again. I turned to face the rock wall so the sun would not be in my eyes. The warmth of the thermal blanket pulled me into a nice sleep.

I was just beginning to have a dream when I felt something hit my ear. Something hit my temple. I opened my eyes and Anita screeched, piercing my ear. All of a sudden, we were being drenched by a downpour! A small cloud was hovering directly over us and literally pouring water on us! We quickly discovered that the thermal blankets were waterproof and we held ours over us as a makeshift tent. Wickersham covered the open top of the glider cart with a sliding roof and Sammy and my dad scooted into the entrance of the cave to get out of the rain.

"Let's move into the cave," I shouted to the other three girls. I had to shout because the sound of the rainfall was deafening. We each held onto the blankets with both hands, keeping them over us the best that we could, and we moved into the cave.

As quickly as the downpour began, it ended and the cloud disappeared. The sky was once again bright and blue above our heads.

"That was the strangest thing I have ever seen," Anita remarked.

"Are you okay?" I asked her. She had been

unconscious or asleep for so long, I was worried about her.

"I am just a little wet, but besides that, I am fine," she said, squeezing water out of her hair.

"Salwa, are you okay?" I asked. "How is your ankle?"

"I feel much better, thank you," she said, holding one of the blankets tightly around herself.

"Anita, glad to see you back among the living," Wickersham said. He sat down on the landing by the glider cart. "Hey, you guys can come out of the cave now. Look how fast the water has dried up!"

"And look how fast our fire was put out," Sammy said. "I must build a new fire." He began to move to the edge of the ledge so he could go get dry supplies for the fire.

"Wait a minute," my dad said.

Sammy stopped.

"Doesn't it strike you as odd, how quickly the rain came and how quickly the cloud disappeared?" my dad asked us, raising one eyebrow.

"That was no ordinary cloud!" Wickersham shouted, slapping his knee.

"What do you mean?" I asked. It looked just like any other cloud, only it was smaller and directly over us, raining only on us and nowhere else.

"It was not a rain cloud moving through and dropping rain in its path," my dad said.

"And it appeared directly above us, dropped water on us, and dissolved," Wickersham said, looking at us with an expression that said, 'I have a secret and you don't know it.'

"Are you saying that was no ordinary cloud?" I asked. I realized that was a dumb question because that was exactly what he had just said.

"That is exactly what I just said!" Wickersham verified, nodding his head wildly.

"Sammy, we better not light another fire," my dad said.

"Why?" Sammy asked.

"That cloud was sent to put out a fire," my dad explained. "Now, whoever sent the cloud may think the fire just started naturally. They may be watching to see if another fire starts. If they see a second fire in this same spot, they could get suspicious and send something else to us."

"Like a missile?" Anita asked. Her voice had an undertone of unbelief.

"Yes, like a missile!" Wickersham yelled at her. "Whatever we do, we do not want to attract the attention of someone who may have weapons that can kill us, sight unseen."

"Sight unseen?" Sammy asked, moving away from the ledge, back towards the rest of us. "If is sight, how can be unseen?" He looked quizzically at Wickersham.

"Oh, never you mind," Wickersham said, dismissing him with a wave of his hand. "Just don't build another fire. That could lead them right to us."

"Understand," my dad said, "we are being extra cautious. The cloud could have been sent automatically, triggered by the smoke. We just do not want to take any chances."

"I think it would be in our best interest to get moving," Wickersham suggested.

"I agree," my dad said. He turned to Wickersham. "Will the glider cart hold Salwa now? Or does it have too much damage?"

"The only damage is on the side," Wickersham said, giving the glider cart a punch. "It should be able to hold her. She's light as a feather, anyway."

"She will be safe?" Sammy asked.

"She will be safe," Wickersham assured him, rolling his eyes.

"What about you, Anita?" my dad asked, turning to face her. "Are you feeling well enough to keep climbing?"

"Why are you asking ME that question?" she said. "Ask these little girls, they are the ones who look like weaklings." She waved her hand in our direction.

Sammy and Wickersham began putting everything into the glider cart, including Salwa.

"I just want to make sure you are completely recovered," my dad said to Anita, with concern.

"Completely recovered?" she demanded, getting in his face. "Completely recovered from WHAT?"

"From your fall," my dad said gently, taking a step back from her. "You really got the wind knocked out of you."

"My fall?" she asked, laughing. "What are you talking about? What has gotten into you, Obiad?"

"Sweetheart, you fell at least ten meters," Wickersham said. He pointed down, in the direction we had come. "Down there."

"You both are crazy," she said, shaking her head. "I did not fall."

She looked as if she really believed what she was saying. Maybe she had hit her head in the fall and lost some of her memory.

"Okay," my dad said, shrugging his shoulders. "Then we are ready to go, onward and upward!"

"What about Nadir?" I asked. "How can he find us?"

"Maybe we will be able to see him when we get to the top of the ridge," my dad said. "Or he can catch up with us when we come down on the other side."

"I guess he will have to," I said, although I was not happy about it. We did not really have a choice. We had to keep moving, and I knew we would have an easier climb while we still had some daylight left than if we waited until the sun set.

"Perhaps he see smoke before rain cloud comes," Sammy said hopefully. "He know where to go to find us."

"Perhaps he did," I said, nodding and hoping.

Wickersham got the glider cart going. As it was hovering in place, he checked to be Salwa was secure. He tested the remote control and when he was satisfied that it was working the way it should, we started on our upward climb. My dad went first, I followed him, and the others were behind us. We had somewhat of a pathway for a short time, winding around big rocks, then the path just ended. We began with the climbing, hand over foot, pulling ourselves up onto big boulders. I watched my dad to see where he was putting his hands and feet. A couple of times, he stopped, searched, and moved sideways to find a path for us to follow.

I was concentrating on taking my next step when I looked to see where my dad was. I couldn't see him!

"Daddy, wait!" I called, trying to find my way. If I put my hand right up there, where could I put my foot?

"What's the holdup?" Wickersham yelled at me.

The glider cart floated up by me.

"Daddy!" I called again.

"I can see your father!" Salwa called. "Climb to next rock!"

That was easy for her to say, hard for me to do. The glider cart disappeared from view. I went to my right and had to go down a couple of steps in order to be able to make the climb. I found an easier way to go, a way that was possible, and as I pulled myself onto a large boulder, I finally made it to the top of the big rocks.

The landscape at this level was so different from what we had seen up to this point. The ground was gray and sandy, and from here I could see what appeared to be the top of the hill. The remainder of the climb looked easy. Not a large rock was in sight, just sand. My dad was a distance away from me, squatting down, holding some sand, letting it slip through his fingers. I wanted to run to him, but after that climb, my legs did not have any energy. The glider cart was hovering near him. I walked to where my dad was and, intending to squat beside him, I flopped down into the sand. My legs did not have the muscle strength to ease me down slowly.

"This is the strangest thing," my dad said, as he examined the sand in his hand.

We were seeing all kinds of the strangest things, it seemed.

"What you see?" Salwa asked, trying to get a look over the edge of the glider cart.

"I cannot figure out how this sand got up here," my dad said.

"I am so glad we made it over those rocks," I said, panting. "It looks like the rest of the way will be quite easy going." My legs were telling me the complete opposite, but I didn't want to admit it.

"I am just curious about this sand," my dad said.

The rest of the group caught up to us.

"So, Maloof, what's the plan?" Wickersham asked, dropping down on the ground beside me.

"Probably billions of years ago, this was a beach, and this sand is left here from that time," Anita said.

"That's one explanation," Wickersham said, pulling a package of nuts out of his pocket. "I'll go with that."

"I don't know," my dad said, taking a closer look at the sand. "It is not like beach sand. Beach sand is made up of tiny granules, tiny bits of shells, that are all different colors. This is all gray, light and dark gray. I don't see any other colors."

"What difference does it make?" Wickersham said. He tossed a nut in the air and caught it in his mouth. I thought about all the time he had had in the shelter to perfect his technique.

"Can the rest of us get something to eat?" Anita asked in a whiny voice.

"Let's just grab something we can eat quickly," my dad said. "I would like for us to cross the summit of this hill before the sun sets."

"I cannot see far down the hill," Sammy said. He

was standing at the edge of a rock, and I knew he was looking for Nadir.

"Do we have to go over the top of the hill?" Anita said, as she got some food and water out of the glider cart. Salwa sat quietly in the cart, just waiting.

"Over the top looks to be a lot shorter than going around," my dad said. "It looks to be sandy going in both directions, but we have no idea how far we would have to walk." He let the rest of the sand filter through his fingers.

I looked to our left and right. Going over the top certainly looked to be a much shorter way than trying to get around this hill. For all we knew, this hill could be miles wide, but we could see the top, and it was not very far away from us. This part of our journey would be a snap, much easier than climbing hand over foot on those boulders we had just covered.

"Here, have a protein bar," Anita said, shoving one into my hand. She distributed them to everyone and we ate quickly.

"Sammy, put on one of the camel pouches," my dad instructed. Sammy lifted one of the water-filled backpacks out of the glider cart and heaved it over his shoulders. Lena helped him strap it onto his back and fasten the latches. Several tubes were coming out of the back, tubes we could use to suck water out of the camel pouch. I went over and tested it. The water was cool and fresh, and I had to restrain myself from drinking too much.

"Okay, is everyone ready to get going again?" my dad asked. "This part of our journey will be easy!"

"Ready!" I said, with renewed strength. I stood to

my feet and jumped up and down a couple of times. Oooh, my legs were telling me that I used some muscles today that had not been worked like that in a long time, if ever.

"Let's get going before it gets dark!" Anita shouted.

"Yes, we want to set up our camp on the other side of the summit," my dad said. "We already know it gets quite cold up here at night."

We started walking and the first few steps were fine. We could have been taking a stroll on a sandy beach — until we reached the incline. There, the sand suddenly got deeper. For each step I took going up, my feet slid back down into the sand almost as far as I had stepped. After taking about twenty steps, I saw that I had gone almost nowhere. My dad was up ahead of me, and I watched to see how he was making such great progress, compared to mine, anyway. He was by no means going uphill fast, he was just covering more ground more quickly than I was.

He was stretching his legs to take longer steps than normal. I tried doing the same, and my muscles cried for me to stop. I could not listen to them; I had to keep going up the hill and I could not let myself slide backwards down the hill.

"This sand is impossible to walk in!" Anita shouted from somewhere behind me.

"Oh, quit your whining and climb!" Wickersham bellowed.

"I told you, you can't tell me what to do!" she yelled.

"Then go back and be comfortable, if you don't want to do the work!" Wickersham said.

"I just might do that!" she said.

Apparently, she did not do that.

My dad was nearing the summit. I was concentrating on taking one more step, sliding back, stretching my leg, and taking one more step, while trying to ignore any conversation behind me, when I heard a familiar voice shout and echo.

"Stop! Bull can!" I heard. I twisted around so I could verify what I was hoping I had heard: Nadir was standing at the bottom of the sandy area!

"Bull can?" I asked.

"Obiad, stop!" Nadir shouted again. "Bull CAN!"

I looked up to my dad, who seemed to be very close to the top. He did not appear to hear Nadir.

"Daddy!" I yelled at the top of my lungs. My voice came out as a little squeak; the air up here must have been very thin. I tried again. "Daddy, stop!"

My dad heard me and stopped. He turned to see why I was yelling.

"Nadir?" he called.

"Bull CAN!" Nadir shouted.

My dad could not hear him.

"Bull CAN!" I relayed. I had no idea why he would be shouting 'bull can' in order to get my dad to stop, but it worked. My dad stopped and I finally caught up to him.

I was breathing hard, trying to get a good breath. I felt like I just could not get the air I needed inside me. My dad was also breathing hard while we rested.

"Why," I said, struggling for breath, "did... Nadir... say... bull... can?"

"Bolcan," my dad said. "It means volcano."

I was terrified. Volcanoes meant hot lava streaming down a mountainside and instantly killing everything in the path.

"I don't see any lava," I said desperately.

My dad inched his way up to the summit of the volcano. While still sitting, he looked over the edge.

"We are on the edge of the crater," he said. "I don't see any lava. It must not be an active volcano. But it's a good thing Nadir stopped me. It is quite a distance down on the other side. We will have to walk around the rim of the crater. A few more steps and I could have slipped right into the crater."

He was sweating, even though the sun was setting and the temperature was dropping rapidly.

"What's the holdup?" Wickersham called, panting, as the rest caught up with us. They were all panting, except for Salwa, who was clutching the edges of the glider cart so that her knuckles were white.

"We are on the edge of a volcanic crater," my dad said calmly. I could tell he did not want the others to panic.

"A volcano?" Anita shrieked.

"That explains the sand," my dad said. "It is not sand, it is volcanic ash."

"Volcanic ash?" Wickersham asked. "But it is just like sand."

"It does seem a lot like sand," my dad agreed. "Only this is ash that has been spewed out from the inside of the volcano."

Nadir finally caught up with us. He was out of

breath, but he was signaling that he wanted to say something.

"You go to north, not straight to west," he said between breaths.

I was just relieved to be sitting and not climbing. My muscles were all so sore and I was so tired, I was hoping we could make camp right there.

"The cloud cover blocked the North Star," my dad explained.

"You came to mountain, faster than going around, but more danger. I see smoke today and I know you come this way. We must go down, off *bolcan*," Nadir insisted. "We go around to north side, can get down fast."

"I can hardly move my legs!" Anita protested, voicing my exact thought. "There is no way I am going to get down fast."

"Follow me," Nadir said, standing and walking up near the edge of the crater. "Take your care!"

We followed him, and I was happy to see a path a few feet wide in places along the edge of the crater. I took one look into the crater, and it did not seem to be so far down; but I did not want to slip down and fall inside it. I kept my focus on the trail, staying as far away from the edge as possible, and I did not allow myself to look into the crater again.

The glider cart was floating along beside Wickersham, not on the crater side, but on the side with the hill. I glanced back to see that Salwa was still gripping the side of the cart, looking as scared as ever.

"What is that sound?" Sammy asked from behind me.

Everyone stopped walking. I heard it, too. Thwup-thuwp-thuwp-thuwp-thuwp-thuwp-thuwp-thuwp. It seemed to be coming from inside the crater.

"It's a helicopter!" Anita shouted. I dared to look inside the crater and way, way down there, about the size of my pinky fingernail, I could see a helicopter moving across the inside surface of the crater. I realized that my initial judgment of the distance down into the crater had been extremely underestimated. That helicopter was at least a mile or so down there.

"Where did it come from?" Wickersham asked, as if any of us would know the answer.

"Perhaps it comes from the place where we are going," Nadir suggested.

"Maybe we are almost there!" I said enthusiastically, completely disregarding the fact that we were walking along on the rim of a crater of a volcano.

"We must keep moving," Nadir said.

We kept moving. We did not have the energy or the breath for conversation, and we soon came to a point where Nadir stopped.

"We go down here," he said, pointing.

"Is that SNOW?" I asked, fascinated. I could not remember ever seeing snow in my life, but this looked like stripes of snow between ridges of the hill.

"We slide on snow," Nadir said.

"Yes!" Wickersham said excitedly. "These suits, we can slide on them!" Without hesitation, he ran down the hillside and jumped onto a strip of snow and began sliding on his bottom. This certainly looked like a much faster way to descend the hill than walking, and in consideration of the condition of my leg muscles, I was looking forward to sliding down, too. It looked like fun!

"We must hurry," Nadir said. "Spread out, you go there, you go there, you wait for her to get down to that rock before you start so you do not crash her."

I slowly made my way down to the top of one of the snow strips, hindered by my muscles that did not want to allow me to take steps in a downward direction. My thighs were aching with every step, so I just kept looking at my goal: the snow. If I could just get there, then I would be able to slide, slide, slide!

"Are you okay, Layla?" my dad called.

I looked over to see him at the top of another snow strip, and I realized he had most likely been waiting for me to get here.

"I'm ready!" I yelled.

"Then let's go!" he said.

With his prompting, I jumped into the snow, landing right on my bottom, and held my feet up, the same way I had seen Wickersham do it. This was really fun! I was sliding down a hill, going faster and faster! I kept my eyes on the snow ahead of me, which seemed to stretch out in an endless ribbon. I quickly learned that I could steer, to an extent, and move to the left or right just by leaning in that direction. My rear end was frozen for a little while, then it became numb, so I just kept riding on it. I was not speeding too fast, just fast enough to make it really fun.

I was sliding down the hill, enjoying myself, when the thought occurred to me: how was I going to stop? The snow slide had to end, and when it did, I would go skidding into — what? Rocks? Sand? Trees?

"Put your feet down to slow down!" my dad yelled, answering my question before I even asked it.

I tried to shove my feet into the snow, but it was too icy on the top and I just kept sliding. I kept trying, and soon my feet hit a weak spot and I went spinning around. Now I was sailing down backwards, just a little more slowly. This would not work for me, so I tried stretching out my legs and digging my heels into the snow. That did not work either. I could not see where I was going, but I had to stop myself before I got to the end of the snow. I made myself straight and stiff, and jerked my legs to my side so I was soon rolling down on the snow.

The snow was not soft and fluffy like I had always been led to believe snow was, but it was hard and crusty. I rolled for a moment until I was finally able to stop. I was cold and I was battered by the snowy hillside, but I was no longer sailing out of control. I took a moment to catch my breath, aware that the air down here was much easier to breathe, although it was still very cold. It felt like icy chips were entering my throat and lungs with every breath I took.

After all that sliding and rolling, I felt a bit dizzy. In the near-darkness, I searched for my companions. My dad had stopped not too far from me, but I could not see any of the others. I stood up to go over to where he was, took one step and my feet flew out from beneath me. The snow was slick! I was once again lying on top of the snow, now with my face on the ground. My dad was just sitting there, so I crawled over to him.

"Are you okay, Daddy?" My rear end was still numb and tingling and my fingers were just about frozen, but I was glad we were away from that crater and not nearly as high as we were just a short time ago.

"I am just regaining my bearings," he said, and I knew exactly what he meant.

"The snow is cold," I said. I was sure he was already aware of that fact, but it was the only thing I could think of at the time.

"Wickersham! Nadir!" my dad cried out. "Where are you? Anita? Sammy?"

All I heard was silence. We were not at the end of our snow slides, so I thought maybe the others were farther down the hill.

"Do you have your flashlight?" I asked my dad.

"I do," he said, and pulled it out of his pocket. He illuminated our surroundings, and I could see that we were approaching the forest, or, in my mind, the top of the tree line. This side of the volcano had ridges and snow instead of the ash section and the rocky section, but the forest apparently went all the way around the base of the hill. We walked on top of the snow, occasionally crashing through the icy crust that covered the powdery stuff underneath it. My shoes were soon soaking wet and my feet were nearly numb when we suddenly came upon the glider cart, parked in the snow. Salwa was sitting inside it, wrapped in thermal blankets.

"You found me!" she exclaimed, as if she had not expected to ever be found.

"Have you seen Lena and Sammy and Nadir?" I asked her.

"I did not see any person after I go down hill," she said. "Cart stop here and I wait."

"Where is Wickersham with the remote control?"

my dad asked.

"I do not know where he goes," she said, looking for him.

"Wickersham!" my dad called again.

"I do not hear him," Salwa said.

"Salwa, let me help you get out of the cart," my dad said, "so we can push it down the hill. It should be able to slide on the snow. Do you think you can walk?"

"I think, yes, I can walk," she said.

My dad easily lifted her out of the glider cart and set her on the crust of the snow. She stood beside the cart, holding onto it for balance while testing the strength of her sore ankle.

"How does it feel?" I asked.

"It not hurt much," she said, putting more weight onto it. "Yes, I can walk."

We began to slide the glider cart on top of the snow towards the forest. Right where the strip of snow ended, the forest began. Darkness had fallen by this time and we could not see a thing in the forest.

"Let's set up a tent and I will light a few lanterns and set them outside, so the others can see where we are," my dad said. "We can go inside and use the thermal blankets to get warm."

"I am ready to get warm!" I said, helping him get the supplies out of the glider cart.

A few minutes later, Salwa and I were inside the tent, huddled close together under thermal blankets while my dad was setting lanterns around the tent and glider cart. I took off my wet shoes. We had one lantern in the tent with us to give us some light.

"Obiad!" a male voice called. "Is that you?"

"Nadir!" my dad shouted. "We have a tent over here!"

"Nadir is here!" Salwa said. "I am very glad he is here. Where is Lena? Where is Sammy?"

"They can't be too far away," I said. "We all came down the same side of the hill, but I didn't see where any of the others went. I was following my dad."

"The cart go very fast and I not see anything," Salwa said. "But we now have Nadir with us here."

Nadir came into the tent. I handed him a blanket and he snuggled up close to Salwa while rubbing his hands together.

"You have not seen Lena and Sammy?" he asked. It sounded like he was trying to keep his teeth from chattering.

"Not since we were on top of the hill," I said.

"No, I have not," Salwa said.

"I am sure they will see the lanterns like you did, Nadir, and come over to the tent," I said, hoping my statement would prove to be true.

"It's starting to snow!" my dad yelled.

"It's snowing?" I asked. My fingers and toes were extremely cold, but I wanted to see what snow looked like as it was falling from the sky.

I peeked my head outside the tent flap and saw the most beautiful sight I had ever seen: in the light of the lanterns, thousands of tiny white flakes were filling the air. Silently, gently, they were drifting toward the ground.

"It's so beautiful!" I said. "But why is it snowing in the summer?"

"The mountain make own weather," Nadir explained, "different from weather around the desert. Cloud come from west and rise above mountain and drop rain and snow on mountain."

"That's kind of interesting," I said, still watching as the snowflakes became larger and more fascinating.

"Now, this is natural snow," my dad said, "not something manufactured, like that rain was, to put out the fire."

"Natural snow," I said, entranced by its splendor, as it fell gracefully to the earth.

Out of the corner of my eye, I thought I saw something moving, but when I turned to look at it, all I could see was the black of the night.

"Helllloooo!" my dad called. He must have seen something, too.

"We find you!" Lena cried.

"Come, quickly, get into the tent and get warm," my dad said.

I backed into the tent as Lena and Sammy tumbled inside with Nadir, Salwa and me. I held out two thermal blankets to them.

"Nadir!" Lena shouted, and put her arms around his neck. Nadir grabbed a blanket and wrapped it around her. I could see a spark between them, and I suddenly felt that Lena had been jealous of me a few days ago when he and I had been spending a lot of time together. I could see that she loved him, much the same way Salwa loved Sammy.

Sammy scooted as close as he could get to Salwa and put his arm around her. He took the other blanket from me and put it around himself and Salwa.

"Where is Anita and other man?" Lena asked, leaning her head on Nadir's shoulder.

I shook my head. "We haven't seen them since we slid down the hill."

"How cart get here without controller?" Sammy asked.

"Layla and her father find me in cart and we push it on top of snow to bring here," Salwa said. "I not know what happen to man with controller."

My dad stuck his head inside the tent. "I need to come in and warm up," he said. "Let's just hope Wickersham and Anita will see the lanterns and find us here."

When he came in, I could feel the cold on him, radiating from him, and I was afraid he might be too cold.

"Daddy, over here," I said, holding open a thermal blanket for him.

He sat beside me and I moved as close to him as possible, so my body heat could help warm him. He put one thermal blanket around himself and I tucked another one around him. His fingers were so very cold, I knew I needed to warm them. I took a deep breath, grabbed his hands, and stuck them underneath my shirt, around my waist. I tried to not think of the cold touching me while I concentrated on the warmth coming from the thermal blanket.

My dad fell asleep almost immediately. I realized that he had been awake for too many hours, and his body had suffered in the cold. I made a pillow out of blankets and clothing and leaned his head against them. I kept his hands against my skin for a while, until his fingers regained heat of their own. All this time he had been doing so much for me, so much for all of us, and now it was my turn to do something for him. I leaned against my dad and in the warmth and quiet of our tent, I soon drifted off to sleep.

"Snow is continue to fall?" I heard Lena ask, as I pulled myself from a deep sleep.

As I opened my eyes, I could see morning had arrived. Nadir was going toward the flap of the tent.

"Good morning," my dad said. As he moved, I also moved, from leaning against him to a sitting position.

"Yes, good morning," I said groggily. I was not really ready to move or even speak, but it was indeed morning.

"What?" Nadir shrieked, pulling his head inside and zipping the tent flap as quickly as he could. "*Bulcan*!"

"The volcano?" my dad asked. "What about it?"

"I see snow fall, but now not snow!"

"Do you mean, ash is coming from the volcano?" my dad asked.

"Yes, very thick ash falls!" Nadir said. "We must stay inside to breathe clean air!"

"We have the masks!" my dad said. "We can wear the face masks, so we can keep going. Otherwise, we will need to stay here. I would not recommend staying, because we don't know how long we might be stuck here."

"We must put on mask, begin to walk," Nadir said.

"How are we going to move the glider cart without the remote control?" I asked.

"We are not going to move it," my dad said. "We will have to carry the supplies we can carry and leave the rest here. Quickly, let's get moving. I'll get the masks. Wait here for a minute."

The night of sleep had completely recharged my dad, and he didn't seem to have any problem with his fingers. I was thankful I had been able to warm them and maybe save them from freezing off his hands, if that were possible.

He left the tent with a shirt wrapped around his nose and mouth and instantly returned with a face mask for each of us.

"We will need to use the goggles," he said, putting on one of the masks.

The other kids and I followed his demonstration and put on our masks the same way. He then pushed a button so goggles came up over the top, and he fastened a strap in the back of his head. We all did the same.

We bundled up the blankets and put them, along with food, water, the other tent and the first aid kit, into backpacks.

"What about Salwa?" I asked. My voice came out all funny, sounding like it was coming through a metal tube. "How can she walk fast enough to keep up with us?"

"I carry Salwa," Sammy said. "She carry backpack."

"Thank you," Salwa said, smiling at him shyly.

"I carry two backpacks," Nadir said, putting a second one on over the one he already was wearing.

As we climbed out of the tent, I was not prepared for the atmosphere. All I could see was white, thicker than the thickest fog. I stood still, not knowing which way to go. This ash was not heavy, like falling sand would be, but it was light and mixing with the air.

Nadir came to me and wrapped a rope around me. As he yanked on a knot, in that funny, metallic voice, he said, "We all tie together with rope so we not get lost. Keep rope tight and follow. Look down to not trip on bush or rock."

We began to move. I was not sure who was in front of me, but I thought probably Nadir was behind me. I was able to see the feet in front of me as they took steps, so I focused all my attention on those two feet, putting my feet in their footsteps as soon as they took their next steps. I was able to breathe using the mask and I was able to see the falling ash. I did not want to imagine how difficult this would be if we had not been wearing masks, because the task would have been impossible.

The ash was piling up on the ground, much the same as it was at the top portion of the mountain, only not nearly as deep. Soon I could see the footprints in front of me, the path I was to follow. Only when I scraped my arm on a tree branch did I realize that we were in the forest. I looked up from the path on the ground to see patches under the trees where ash was not falling and I tripped over a small bush. I again concentrated on each step, one at a time, as I followed the person in front of me, step by step, one step at a time.

The person in front of me stopped, so I stopped. I was able to take my eyes off the path, and I saw that we were deep in the forest, so deep that only a bit of ash was able to penetrate the tree covering. We were all quiet as we looked at our forest companions who had come here for shelter: several deer, a moose, many rabbits and a couple of foxes. They stared at us and we stared at them for a few minutes until we began moving again.

The wildlife was so picturesque, I was reluctant to leave so quickly. I wanted to stand there and stare at them all day, to become friends with them and live with them in the forest. The tug of the rope around my waist reminded me that this would not be possible. We needed to keep moving.

After just a few steps, we stopped again. The first person in our line, which I now saw was my dad, stepped out of the rope loop and ran over to a bush. He squatted down to examine something that I could not see from where I stood. The rest of us, still connected to each other, moved slowly toward him.

My dad pulled off his mask. "It's Wickersham and Anita!" he shouted. "I mean, it's their clothes, but they are not here!" He quickly replaced his mask and returned to his place as the leader of our line.

I did not want to ask the question, but I just knew they had been eaten by wild animals. Suddenly, I was in a hurry to leave the forest as I realized my almost-friends, the animals, were not to be our cherished companions. I did not let myself imagine what other kinds of animals were there, the carnivorous types.

We moved out of the area very quickly. The next section of forest was dense, and not as much ash was falling there. After walking for quite some time, we were out of the forest. I was so relieved to see that we had come out of the ash fallout area. The air was clear and the sky was blue. We took off our masks as soon as we stopped in the clearing. I felt the heat of the day smack my face. After all the cold weather and snow we had encountered, the heat felt very good, as I let it seep into my skin.

"I need some water," Nadir said, pulling the straw-thing from the camel pouch on his back and taking a big drink. We stepped out of the rope that was tying us together and Dad put it in his pack.

"Which way next?" my dad asked, after he had taken a drink of water.

"We must be very close," Nadir said, wiping his mouth with his sleeve.

The rest of us also took a drink of water. In such a strange place as this, doing something normal like drinking water was very refreshing.

I looked up to see where Nadir and my dad were looking and I wanted to cry. Ahead of us stood an enormous snow-covered mountain, much larger than the hill, the volcano, we had just climbed. The height of the mountain, the amount of snow and the sheer faces of rock told me that we would not be able to climb over this one.

"We are not going to try to climb over that mountain, are we?" I asked, trying to keep the panic from my voice.

"We go around," Nadir said. "City must be on other side. We are close. My original path was, we go around *bulcan* and hills, much farther to walk. Now, just one mountain we walk around. Very easy, take two or three days, maybe four days."

I wondered if the rest were as thankful as I was when I heard that we were merely going to walk around a mountain instead of trying to climb over it.

"Let's stop here and eat," my dad said.

He didn't have to tell us twice. We instantly dropped to the ground, right where we were. Everyone must have been as tired and stressed as I was. I sat on a rock and took another drink of water. Lena took some food out of the backpack she was carrying and gave us each a protein bar and a packet of dried fruit. We ate our snacks pensively, without speaking. I did not want to think about Wickersham and Anita; instead I looked at the mountain and imagined what it was going to be like when we walked around it.

The mountain was beautiful, with three peaks that were covered with snow. The snow seemed to be flowing down the steep slope and ended above a layer of huge black and gray rocks. Some of the rocks were shimmering and I assumed they must have been wet, perhaps from melting snow or recent rain (that mountain probably made its own weather, just like the volcano did). The reflections of the sun on the rocks on what I guessed to be the south side gave the mountain a majestic look. Below the rock level was a ring of trees, another thick, lush forest surrounding the base of the mountain. From where I sat, I could imagine a path around the mountain, through the forest. On the other side of the mountain, we would finally reach our destination: a city with more than one thousand people!

We finished eating and my dad told Nadir to take the lead. We collected our supplies and prepared for the next leg of our journey. Nadir turned to face the rest of us before he started walking.

"We walk to edge of forest and set up camp," Nadir said. "We need to rest when sun very hot. We start to walk again after sun go down. Sammy, you are okay with Salwa?"

"Yes, I am okay," he said, hoisting her up a little higher on his back. "Salwa, you are okay?"

"Yes, thank you," she said, hugging her arms around his chest.

We started walking with renewed energy. Nadir was now in the lead with Lena by his side, Sammy and Salwa were behind them, and my dad and I brought up the rear.

"Daddy," I said, "did I tell you today that I love you?" I had a flash of a memory of long ago when we would ask that of each other every day.

"You are telling me now," my dad said, "and I love you, too, my darling daughter."

I smiled, warmed by the feeling of my dad's love.

"Do you think Uncle Pierce will be in this city where we are going?" I asked.

"We cannot be sure, but I believe that he is," my dad said with confidence.

"I think so, too," I said. "When we heard that he survived The Great Devastation, the bombings, I knew that he was still alive even now. It is the weirdest thing. All these years, I have been told that you and Uncle Pierce were dead. There was no question about it. Those were the facts that had been presented to me. But inside my heart, my deepest heart, my secret heart, I felt that God had done a miracle and you were still alive. My logical self had to accept what they were saying, but my real self, inside me, could not accept that. I could never tell anyone that I thought you were alive, because most of the people in the Complex had a fantasy that their loved ones were still alive. We were only allowed to speak of what we were told was the truth. Did I tell you, they could listen to everything we said? The whole place was filled with hidden microphones."

"That must have been terrible for you," my dad said sympathetically.

"We just got used to it," I said, shrugging my shoulders. "It was the only way of life we knew, after a while. But now, after having this freedom we have here, I don't see how I could ever go back to living that way."

"In this city where we are going, I hope they don't have that kind of control over the citizens."

"Do you think they will have technology?" I asked.

"I don't know."

"What about electricity?"

"I do not know that either."

"What do you think?" I turned to see his face. Perhaps I could read his real answer in his expression.

"Yes, actually I do think they have electricity and technology," my dad said, nodding his head. "One thousand people or more who were able to come together after the bombings would most likely have been able to either bring those things with them to this city, or they would be able to create them."

"That is what I think, too," I agreed. My dad had a very logical mind, in addition to a connection with God, and usually what my dad believed was true.

The group stopped walking. We were about halfway to the edge of the forest.

"Obiad!" Nadir called.

"Yes? What is it?"

"Up there, looks like man-made path!" He pointed

straight ahead of us to a definite path through a grassy area that was leading up to the forest; yet it stopped a few meters before it got to the forest.

"Let's go see what it is," my dad said.

We began walking faster, despite the rising temperature. We were curious to see this path, to walk on it. Why was it there? Where did it go? Why did it end right there? Perhaps it was an optical illusion and something was hiding the rest of the path.

In just a few minutes, we were at the edge of the path, where the long grassy area began and was split by the path, which was a couple of meters wide. It was either well-trampled by lots of foot traffic or it had been made with some kind of a machine.

"We follow to end of path then we set up camp under trees," Nadir said, stepping onto the path.

We all followed him and were able to make very good time while on the path. Just as we were approaching the end of the path, a loud noise stopped us in our tracks.

CHAPTER 11

What looked to be the end of the path was actually a giant door going into the ground! The door was opening toward us! I instinctively took a step backward, but I could not run.

Two men with shields and spears stepped out of the ground as soon as the door opened. They immediately took a defensive stance — or was it an offensive stance? They held up their shields and their spears.

"Who sent you?" one of the men demanded.

My dad stepped in front of all of us kids. "We walked here on our own. No one sent us."

"That is impossible!" the second man said, pointing his spear at us. "No one can walk here! Who sent you?"

"Look, these are just kids," my dad said, opening his palm toward us. "One of our girls is injured."

"We will bring you inside," the first man said. "First you give us your weapons." He put down his shield to hold out one hand. His other hand was still ready with the spear, but at least he wasn't pointing it at us.

"We don't have any weapons," my dad said. "We come in peace. These are children!"

Sammy shifted Salwa on his back and both men jumped.

"What are you doing?" the second man asked, leaning toward Sammy.

"She slips and I help her," Sammy said.

Both men looked Sammy up and down, and apparently they were satisfied with his answer.

"Do you swear that you have no weapons?" the first man asked.

"We all swear we have no weapons," my dad said, holding up his right hand, as if that would make his statement more true.

"Okay, then," the second man said. "We will take you inside. You all stay together and don't try anything."

We walked through the opening in the ground and went down about ten steps into an enormous tubular hallway. Lanterns were posted along the walls, revealing that the hallway was at least four meters tall and wide. The floor was flat, but the walls and ceiling were curved, something like the inside of a giant pipe. The entrance was at one end of the tube where we were standing, and from there, I couldn't see where we were going, just that we had a long hallway ahead of us.

We began walking straight ahead, our only option. There was nothing to see along the way, no writing or notices on the walls, no windows, no doors, no other people. As we were going along, we came to an intersecting hallway, off to our right. This one also had curved walls and ceiling, but was about twice as wide and brightly lit at the end. I stopped to look, to be sure my eyes were not playing tricks on me, but no, they were not. It was actually there: a restaurant! Beneath the ground, inside a tube, were stools at a bar, tables and chairs, the scent of food cooking, people sitting and eating! One man was eating ice cream. A woman was eating a sandwich and two people were sitting at the bar sipping drinks. The walls were brightly painted white with red swirls, the floor was white tile and the furniture was all shiny red.

"Get moving!" one of the men shouted, and I started

walking again, reluctant to take my eyes off that scene.

A couple of people looked up from their meals with indifference at us. Their existence was so strange to me, but they did not seem the least bit curious about us.

We continued walking down the tunnel and we passed another restaurant, this one dimly lit with many small tables and lots of plants. We then passed an opening that said it was a cinema. A poster listed movies currently playing in 3D, along with coming attractions. I recognized all the titles; these were movies that had been made in the Time Before. Everyone who lived at the Complex knew that the technology to make movies no longer existed. Even if the equipment were to be created again, we just did not have enough people left on earth for some to spend all of their time on fictional pastimes. Each person had a job to do in order to support the entire community.

Finally, we arrived at the end of the hallway. One of the men who was accompanying us put his hand on a pad beside the enormous door. The pad glowed a bright green and the door slid open, sideways, disappearing into the wall.

We stepped into the largest room I had ever seen. This room was at least ten times bigger than the common area of the Complex, although the ceiling was not quite as high. The room was dimly lit and filled with people working at computers, or so they appeared to be. Many people were sitting at monitors while others had hand-held devices. Screens covered the walls, many of them dark, and many of them showing scenes of outside. My eye went directly to a close-up of a volcano spewing ash. Another screen had a view of a forest, and I wondered if someone had seen us on a monitor and sent these two guys to greet us. The room had no windows.

"Come this way," one of the men said.

He led us up a stairway, at least a hundred steps, and through a passageway to another door. Again, he put his hand on a panel, the panel glowed green, and the door slid open. He took us into another very large room. This room had a large window that overlooked a forest, and I realized we were inside the huge mountain! I had seen this window from a distance, a window that was camouflaged to look like a huge rock.

"Give me your packs," one man said, reaching out his hand to us. "Hurry up, give them to me."

Sammy finally put Salwa on the ground. The rest of us took off the packs and camel pouches we were wearing and handed them to the man. The two men searched our packs and then tossed them back to us.

"Do you have any weapons?" the man asked.

"No," my dad said.

"How can you walk across the desert and expect to survive without weapons?" one man asked.

"First of all, we traveled with much prayer. Secondly, why would we need a weapon in the desert?" my dad asked. "We didn't expect to see anyone."

"Why are you here?" the other man demanded.

"We heard about a city with more than a thousand people," I said. "We were in a very small group, so we thought we would join up with the people of the city."

My dad gave me a look that told me I should have let him do all the talking. He smiled and his face softened. Although I had spoken out of turn, I had been telling the truth.

"We have nearly three thousand people in our city," the man said. "We may be able to accept a few more. Where are the others?"

I was wondering if he knew there had been others because they had been spying on us, or if he was just trying to get information from us. I also wondered if he knew about the others we had left back at the shelter at the Four Quadrants, and those at the Complex. This time, I kept my mouth shut.

"We lost two people on the journey," my dad said. "We came down the side of the volcano, we slid down on the snow, and when we got to the bottom, we couldn't find the other two in our group, a man and a woman."

"You are saying you lost a man and a woman on your journey?" one man asked, raising one eyebrow at my dad.

"Yes," my dad said, nodding his head, "that is what I am saying."

I wanted to mention that we had found their clothing, but I decided to just keep quiet.

"Now, there are, let's see: one, two, three, four, five, six of you," the man counted, pointing to each of us in turn, "one adult male and five kids."

I could see Nadir about to protest his status as a kid, but he looked at me and he didn't say anything. Lena looked scared — her eyes were about as big as the face of my Wat-Com — so I tried to give her a reassuring look. I knew from my experience at the Complex that intruders were to be questioned. They would most likely be released into some Outside community, unless they could contribute usefully to the good of the Complex, but they would not be hurt. I was confident that any society that had come together after The Great Devastation would be friendly; or, at least, not hostile.

"Did anyone who lives here come from the Four Quadrants?" my dad asked.

The two men stood at attention and looked at each other. One nodded at the other, who quickly left the room.

"So… you do know someone from the Four Quadrants?" my dad asked, leaning toward the one man who stayed with us in the room. "You didn't live there at any time, did you?"

"No, sir, I did not. I did not live there at any time." The man stayed standing erect, looking straight ahead.

I wanted to say, "Four Quadrants, Four Quadrants, Four Quadrants, Four Quadrants!" to see what he would do, to see if he could stand any straighter, but I did not say a thing. I smiled at the thought, though.

"But you do know someone from there?" my dad asked.

"You will have your answer shortly," the man said.

Just as he spoke the door slid open. Two men wearing uniforms entered with the other man we had already met.

"These are the intruders?" the taller man asked, looking at each of us kids. He seemed disappointed, as if we were a flock of geese or something, and that he had been bothered for no reason. "Just get them out of here," he said, dismissing us. "They have no business here with us."

CHAPTER 12

He had a hat that covered much of his head, but I saw my dad staring at him. The man did not even look at my dad, but I knew that voice! I knew that face!

"Uncle Pierce!" I shouted.

He turned on his heel to face me. On his face was a look of shock. I did not wait to follow the proper military protocol — I jumped over to him and gave him a big hug.

He stood there, stiff as a board, and I realized that he did not recognize me. After all, he had not changed much, he was just thinner and his hair was getting gray instead of jet black, as it had been. In nine years, I had grown up, from a child into a young woman.

"It's me, Layla!" I said, still hugging him.

"Pierce," my dad said, reaching out his hand to him.

For the first time, Uncle Pierce looked at my dad. His face softened, back to that uncle I had known, melting away the military indifference.

"Obiad? How is this possible? You died in the air raid!" He let me keep hugging him while he reached out to grab my dad's hand and we all hugged together. "Were you able to escape with Moon and Sun?"

"Excuse me, sir, but how can a man escape with the moon and the sun?" the other soldier, or whatever the man in uniform was, said to Uncle Pierce.

My dad and Uncle Pierce laughed. It was so good to hear their laughter again! I had never expected to hear them laugh with each other until we all would meet in heaven, but here we were, still on earth, and they were laughing together.

"I did not escape with them," my dad said, ending our group hug. "Layla was on the plane with them, and she just recently found me."

I beamed at my Uncle. My dad and I were actually here, with part of our family! Uncle Pierce looked so sharp in his uniform.

"So, they did escape safely!" Uncle Pierce asked. "I am so thankful to hear that. Where are they now? Are they here, with you?" He took another look at Nadir, Sammy, Salwa and Lena as if to see if he had somehow overlooked his wife and sister-in-law in our group.

"No, they are not here," my dad said.

I could see the disappointment spread across Uncle Pierce's face. "Of course not," he muttered.

"We left on the plane, just like you told us to do," I said, "and then after we landed, we were separated when things were getting organized After The Great Devastation, what you called the air raid. They, the leaders of the community, took me to the Complex, a highly structured society, and I don't know where they took Mom and Aunt Moon."

"But they are still alive," my dad added.

"You have seen them?" Uncle Pierce asked hopefully.

"No, but I know for sure they are alive," my dad said. He sounded so positive, I believed him, even though he had no real evidence.

"Obiad, how is it possible that you survived the air raid?" Uncle Pierce asked, turning to my dad.

"I was saved by the Word of God," my dad said, "literally. I was in the warehouse getting ready to distribute the Bibles when I heard the first bomb. I hit the floor and the Bibles protected me. I woke up some time later, surrounded by Bibles. I was able to get out and I saw that all of the Four Quadrants had been destroyed. I searched for weeks and never found another survivor."

"You didn't know about the bomb shelter," Uncle Pierce said. "I didn't either, well - I knew it was in progress, but didn't know how ready it was - until I woke up down there with a handful of other people. I had just called my wife and told her to meet me at the plane and I was on my way to your office to bring you with me. I had no idea you were at the warehouse, but it didn't matter because we couldn't have made it to the plane anyway. I thought we had a least a few more minutes, but I was wrong. Before I could even get out of the building, I heard an explosion and something hit me on the head. Next thing I knew, I woke up and I was underground and they said we had to stay there because of the toxicity in the air. We stayed there for years before we started to venture out. After we left, we tried to use our communicators to contact the ones back at the bomb shelter, but we couldn't get through to them. We didn't know if they were still alive. After wandering around in the desert for quite some time and not finding any place to stay, we met some guys from here, and we ended up staying here. We kept trying to communicate with no success, until just the other day when we finally got a signal from them. We sent our location and not much more when we saw on the tracking screens that the shelter was bombed by missiles.

"I apologize for any hostility or inconvenience when you were brought here. We had to assume that any strangers who were approaching us may be the ones who launched the missiles. We have not had any contact with any other city or society. Do you know who launched the missiles or where they came from?"

My dad shook his head. "Some of us were planning to stay underground for awhile, but we had come outside and we were testing out one of the glider carts. That saved our lives. We followed the cart clear across two quadrants, and while we were there, we heard the explosions and we took off."

"Come, let us have a seat," Uncle Pierce said, waving his hand toward a couple of couches in the corner of the room. "How did you get to the shelter in the first place? And Layla, how did you get there?"

"A few months after the Four Quadrants was destroyed," my dad said, settling into his seat, "I met up with some nomads who were looking for food. I took them to the remains of one of the warehouses and we were able to get enough food from there to survive for years. We set up our camp not too far from the Four Quadrants, in a spot that was out of the wind."

Uncle Pierce nodded while watching my dad intently. "Yeah, that was some fierce wind in that valley."

"I stayed with them for years, until one day recently, a miracle happened," my dad said, smiling from ear to ear. "Layla walked into our camp. All of us were wearing robes, the only clothing we had to protect us from the desert heat. My brilliant daughter had the idea for us to find some 'normal' clothing for the other kids — we had six youngsters in our group — so some of us went up to the Four Quadrants and started digging. We uncovered one of the entrances to the shelter and soon we found the people who were living there: Wickersham, Anita, Beezeeneck…" he was counting them on his fingers. He stopped and looked to me for the names of the others.

"Dr. Conrad-Bean," I said, proud that I had remembered his name, then sad because of his probable fate.

"And... who else was there?" my dad asked, looking at us kids.

"Salmoony!" Nadir said.

The rest of us nodded.

"That was all, just five," I said.

"Salmoony, what a character," Uncle Pierce said, with a chuckle. "How is he doing? Oh, and how is Anita? She, well, anyway, how is she doing?"

"We don't know," my dad said. "She was with us, but a couple of nights ago — or was it just last night? — we got separated. She was with Wickersham." He omitted the part about finding their clothes in the forest.

"She was with Wickersham?" Uncle Pierce asked, laughing loudly. "They hated each other! I can just imagine them, having to be alone together. I don't know which one I feel more sorry for, Wickersham or Anita!"

"We are not sure what happened to Salmoony," my dad said, his tone serious. "The few of us were away from the shelter, and it looked like the bomb landed right near the entrance. Quite a few of the men from our tribe, the ones I was living with—"

"And our fathers!" Lena added, with a pained expression on her face.

"Yes, and their fathers, were all inside the shelter at the time of the explosion," my dad said.

"I am sorry to hear that," Uncle Pierce said.

"We are hoping they survived," Nadir said. I could see that he did not have much hope in his expression.

"Yes, of course," Uncle Pierce said.

I was hoping to be able to tell him my part of the story, how I had come from the Complex to the Four Quadrants and found my dad, but I did not get the opportunity. Another man in uniform entered the room.

"Sir?" he asked. I got the feeling that Uncle Pierce was an important officer.

Uncle Pierce stood and nodded at the man. He turned to us. "We have plenty of room for you to stay here," he said. "By the way, are you planning to stay here, or do you have another destination?"

"This was our destination," my dad said, "but we didn't realize the city was hidden inside a mountain."

"I was surprised when I learned that this city has been inside this mountain for more than a hundred years," Uncle Pierce said.

"A hundred years?" I asked. My mouth dropped open.

"It was built by some survivalists in the previous century," Uncle Pierce said. "They were preparing for a world war, and they found this mountain that had caverns and tunnels all through it. They began to dig out rooms while reinforcing the outer structure, and they loaded it up with technology, solar panels and supplies."

"I remember hearing about it," Nadir said, nodding his head knowingly. "We thought it was all story. We did not believe it really exist."

"It is really amazing," Uncle Pierce said. I could

tell he was trying to leave the room, probably to attend to his duties, but he was so enthusiastic about our conversation. "This city cannot be seen or detected from the outside. All transmissions are cloaked so there is no way to track them, even if anyone has the technology to use satellite trackers. The city is truly hidden."

"Sir?" the uniformed man at the door said again.

"If you will excuse me, I need to go," Uncle Pierce nodded toward the man at the door, "but Ryder here will show you to your quarters. I will join you for our meal in about an hour. Ryder, we can dine in the Apple Tree Room. I will see you there."

"Bye, Uncle Pierce," I said, springing up to give him a hug. He was not at all expecting me, and he gave a little laugh as I grabbed him.

"Layla, I am so happy you are here," he said, returning my hug. "And the rest of you, too," he added.

Uncle Pierce and the other man who came with him left the room and Ryder stood at attention at the door. I looked at my dad, who motioned to the others to stand up and get ready to follow Ryder to our quarters.

"This way," Ryder said, leading us out of the room.

We followed him down a hallway then we turned into another hallway. We walked by about a hundred doors that had numbers on them before he stopped in front of door number 242.

"This room is for the young ladies," he said, putting his hand on the panel beside the door. As it began to glow green, he held his hand there for a few seconds. "You, put your hand on this panel," he said to me.

I put my hand on the panel until the green glow flashed and he told me to remove it. He then had

Lena and Salwa do the same thing. I assumed he was programming the device to open by sensing our hands. When we were finished, he again put his hand on the panel to open the door. We all followed him into the room.

The first thing I noticed about the room was that it had a window. We were high up on the mountain now but it was hard to see anything out the window. I wondered if it were dark outside, or if the window had a dark tint to it. I turned my attention to Ryder, who was beginning to speak.

"This is your main room, there is your wash room which leads to the bedroom. The closet holds your linens, towels, personal items and clothing. If you have any needs or questions, use the communication device on that wall. For your entertainment, we have the electronic book collection as well as the viewing device on the wall."

I saw four devices on a shelf, thinking that they were not much of a collection, and then I looked at the giant screen on the wall, the one he called the viewing device. As Ryder was taking my dad and the boys out of our room, I walked into the bedroom. As I entered, a warm light illuminated the room, but I didn't see any light fixtures. It was as if the walls and ceiling had just gotten brighter and they were now glowing. I did not see any beds or a closet, but I did notice small panels on the wall, camouflaged so they were hard to see, and I put my hand on one, just to see what would happen.

I saw a glowing reddish color strip on one of the walls, and a bed slid out of it. I touched the next panel and a bed came out above the first one.

"How you did do that?" Lena asked. I hadn't noticed

that she had followed me into the room. I glanced through the doorway and saw Salwa was sitting on a comfortable looking couch with her foot resting on a small stool.

"I just put my hand on this panel," I said, touching the first panel again. The bed slid back into the wall and disappeared. I examined the wall to find the opening where the bed had appeared, but I could not see even a line on the wall.

"I can try?" Lena asked.

"Sure, just touch one of these panels," I said, pointing to the small bank of panels near the doorway.

Lena touched one of the other panels and an opening appeared across the room. I walked over and looked into it — a closet with shelves full of clothing, towels, brushes, toothbrushes, blankets, and sheets, among other things. I wondered if the beds could automatically change their own sheets. After all, wouldn't the forward-thinking people who had designed this place need to spend their time doing things other than changing sheets on the beds?

"Here is the closet," I announced, turning back to Lena.

Lena touched another panel and another bed popped out of the wall, this one on the other side the room, across from the first two beds.

"How many beds?" she asked.

I shook my head. "I don't know. Let's find out. Let's try all of the panels and see what they do."

She put her palm on the panels, one at a time. We discovered the room had four beds, two closets (the other one was full of clothing of all sizes and colors), and a viewing screen.

"Salwa, come and see," Lena called to her.

Salwa wobbled into the bedroom and looked. "Top bed!" she exclaimed. I assumed she meant 'top bunk.' Her face grew wide with a grin, then she frowned. "No top bed for me."

"You can have one as soon as your ankle gets better," I promised. I was hoping Lena wanted a top bunk because I really did not want one, but I would take one if she needed to be on the bottom bunk. We left the beds out and the doors to the closet open so everything was accessible without us having to go to all the trouble of touching a panel to get to what we needed.

After we checked out the wash room and found everything in order, including a nice shower, I wanted to tell my dad about our room. I realized that we didn't know which room was his, or if he was even on the same level as we were. We would have to wait until he wanted to come back to us.

"I guess we have to wait for the guys to come back here," I said, "since we don't know where they are."

Lena and Salwa exchanged glances and I thought I saw a touch of panic in their expressions.

"We do not know their room," Lena said.

"Let's just relax and get comfortable here," I said. "I would love to take a shower, wouldn't you?"

They again exchanged glances. This time they looked very uncomfortable.

"You take shower where?" Salwa asked, with a puzzled look on her face.

"In the wash room," I said, then I laughed. "No, I

am not going to take it anywhere. I mean to say, 'I am going to have a shower.'"

They both smiled at me, not getting the joke.

"I like to sleep," Salwa said.

"Oh, yes, of course," I said. "Pick whichever bed you want, and that one will be yours."

We all went into the bedroom. Lena and Salwa stretched out on the two lower bunks, so I had my choice of one of the upper bunks. I would select one later; right then, all I could think about was a nice, hot shower.

I had to settle for a medium-warm shower, but it was still very nice. I washed the ash, dust, dirt and snow residue out of my hair, but before I could rinse out the soap, the water turned itself off. I touched the panel again to turn on the water, but nothing happened. I was standing there with my head covered in soapy suds and the shower was no longer releasing any water. I crossed the room to the sink and touched the panel there. Water came out of the faucet and I stuck my head under it. I had to do this five times in order to get all the soap out of my hair. When I finished, I began shivering, so I wrapped myself in one of the towels I had brought from the closet. The towel must have been made of some miracle substance, because it was so warm, but not too hot. The water on my body just evaporated into the towel, but the towel did not become wet, it just stayed warm.

I began to get sleepy. I tiptoed into the bedroom where Lena and Salwa were both sleeping. I found some clothing that looked to be my size in a nice deep red color and put it on. I wanted to get onto one of the top bunks, but I didn't see how I could do that without bothering either Lena or Salwa by stepping on a lower bunk. I walked around to the end of the beds and a ladder appeared out of nowhere, or maybe from the top bunk, and I climbed it. I was not at ease sleeping on a top bunk, but it was extremely comfortable, and it was very warm. The bed seemed to meet my body at just the exact right temperature to make me fall asleep almost immediately.

When I awakened, the room was very dark, so dark that I could not see if Lena and Salwa were still in their beds. I wanted to find out if we had missed the meal — I was not sure if it would have been breakfast or dinner, but I was hungry. I scooted to the end of my bed and as I moved, even just that little bit, the lights in the room began to glow, just slightly, enough for me to see that Lena and Salwa were still asleep. I could also see that the ladder was now gone, so I prepared to ease myself down to the floor, but suddenly that was not necessary. As I approached the end of the bed, the ladder again appeared, so I climbed down the same way I had come up.

I was a surprised when I saw in the mirror the crisp, clean clothing I was wearing, having forgotten that I had changed. I had been wearing the same outfit for so long, I almost did not recognize myself in anything else.

I wandered into the main room and looked out the window. Now the outside looked to be much darker than it had been earlier, and I was very curious to know what time it was. I did not see any clocks or anything to indicate the time or date. I was wondering how I was going to get in touch with my dad when I was startled by some movement to my left. The giant entertainment device was glowing a deep blue color and then some yellow letters began to form words on the screen.

"Layla, Lena, Salwa, we will meet you at your room to go to eat. Wait for us there," were the words on the screen.

Where else could we go? I didn't even know if we could get out of this room. I went over to the door and put my right palm on the panel. Nothing happened. I tried my other hand. Still, nothing happened. We were trapped inside these rooms!

I must have cried out because Lena ran out of the bedroom.

"You are okay?" she asked.

"We can't get out!" I said, trying unsuccessfully to calm my voice. I again put my palm on the panel and nothing happened. "See? The door won't open!" I pounded on the panel, as if that would somehow jar it into working, but still, the door did not open. I looked at Lena and she must have seen crazy eyes on my face because I was really scared.

CHAPTER 13

"Did you push off lock?" Lena asked, looking toward the panel.

"The lock?" I asked. I looked near the panel and saw a small red panel that said "Lock." I pushed it with one finger and it glowed green. I then put my palm on the panel near the door, it glowed green, and the door slid open.

"We must push off lock before open door," Lena said with a smile.

"Yes, yes, we can't open it when it's locked," I said, nodding, as if I had known all along.

My dad, Nadir, and Sammy came around a corner and saw us standing in the doorway.

"Ready to go eat?" my dad asked.

"Yes, we are ready," I said. "Lena, do you want to get Salwa?"

Lena went to the bedroom and returned a moment later. "Salwa want to sleep now. I can bring her food?"

"I'm sure we will be able to bring her some food," my dad said.

"Do you know where to go?" I asked. As I looked up and down the hallway, it all looked the same: rows of doors with numbers on both sides, as far as I could see.

"Pierce sent me directions on our big screen to where we are to meet him," my dad said.

"And I transfer to computer," Nadir said, holding up the computer, to confirm his statement. "I have map of entire mountain city in computer. Mountain city has fourteen levels!"

"Fourteen levels?" I asked.

"Fourteen levels?" Lena repeated.

"Yes, fourteen levels," he confirmed, nodding enthusiastically. "I show you later, when we arrive."

As soon as Lena and I stepped into the hallway, our door closed.

"Remember, we are in room number 242," I said to Lena.

"I have in computer," Nadir said, holding up the computer.

"Well, if we lose you or if you lose the computer, we need to know our room number."

"Yes, you are good thinking," he said.

"Salwa not feeling good?" Sammy asked. He had a look of real concern on his face.

"She very tired," Lena said.

I was fascinated by the action of the lighting as we walked down the hallway. The area just ahead of us would get a little bit brighter and after we passed through, it would be come darker. The lighting in the hallway reminded me of a moving, glowing ball. When I looked way behind us, the hallway was very dark, as it was way in front of us. However, right where we were at the moment, the lighting was bright and glowing around us. The change was so subtle as we traveled; it was not a harsh or disturbing brightening and dimming, but very peaceful and calming.

Nadir led us down corridors, up stairs, across walkways and through an area that made me think of the mall at the Four Quadrants. This area had a wide walkway dividing two rows of shops, restaurants, hair-managing stations and entertainment centers, all decorated with colored lights which also grew brighter as we walked by them. All kinds of plants were growing everywhere, and I looked up to see huge windows on the high ceilings, although it looked dark outside the windows. Between the windows, I recognized grow lights, similar to some we had back at the Complex, lights to promote plant growth.

"We need to go over there," Nadir said, pointing to a door across the way from us.

We went through the door and entered what looked to be a work area, similar to the one we saw when we first arrived at this hidden mountain city, only smaller. Only a few people were working, and I saw Uncle Pierce walking toward us.

"I see you had no trouble finding this room," he said. He reached out to give me a hug, and it almost seemed like nine years apart had only been but a few days. "We can go to eat at the Apple Tree Room. I think you will like it. We will need to go up several more levels, but it has windows facing east and we will be able to see the sunrise. You won't believe how beautiful the sunrise looks from up there. Hey, wasn't there another girl with you? You didn't lose her, did you?"

I released him from our hug. "No, she stayed in the room to rest. I hope we can bring her some food?" I was a bit apprehensive asking him, since back at the Complex, they discouraged us from taking food to our pods; unless, of course, my Comgen friend, Kenrick, wanted to do it. He was able to give himself permission to do anything, since he had full access to all of the computer systems.

"Oh, sure, no problem!" Uncle Pierce said. "We have everything well-ordered here, but we also have a lot of freedom. As long as everyone abides by the rules, we won't have any problems."

"Rules?" Nadir asked. "How we know these rules?"

"When you return to your quarters, you can read them or listen to them on your viewing device at your convenience."

"This is quite some setup," my dad said, looking around the room.

"This is where I work," Uncle Pierce said. "This is not the highest of the rankings, but we are pretty high up here. Obiad, I can probably get you a job up here, if you want. You boys, you can work downstairs. You can have your pick of positions. We have so many vacancies."

"What about us?" I asked. "What will we do?" I was referring to us girls, but I assumed Uncle Pierce knew that.

"We can find something for you to do," he said patronizingly.

His tone of voice made me afraid that he was going to say I could wash some dishes or clean some rooms, but I didn't ask any more questions about that. I figured we were newcomers. Even though I had held an essential position at the Complex — or I had been led to believe I did, anyway — I was just a new person here, and I would do whatever they needed me to do until I could prove that I was able to do a greater job, something important. Uncle Pierce probably still saw me as a little girl. I just nodded my head and gave him the best smile I could at the time.

"This place is incredible," my dad said. "Are you some kind of general or something? Are you the one in charge?"

Uncle Pierce laughed. "I am not in charge, but I have earned a nice position here. They look very highly on pilots in this city."

"What do you call this city?" I asked. "I mean, does it have a name?"

"Of course it has a name," Uncle Pierce said. "The name is 'Mountain Veil,' or 'Mountain Veil City.' A good name, isn't it?"

"What this mean, Mountain Veil?" Nadir asked.

"It means it's hidden by the mountain, doesn't it?" I asked.

"Exactly," Uncle Pierce said, nodding his head.

"Only it's not really a city hidden BY the mountain," I said. "It is actually a city hidden IN the mountain."

Uncle Pierce laughed. "Only you would come up with something like that."

"That's true," my dad agreed, smiling at me. "You always were such a stickler for words and their meanings."

"I'm not being a stickler," I protested. "That's just how it is."

My dad put his hand across my shoulder. "That's my girl," he said.

"How big is this place?" Nadir asked.

"You saw the mountain when you were walking here," Uncle Pierce said.

"Of course, so large, we must see it," Nadir said.

"The city goes nearly to the top of the mountain, and it fills the entire mountain," Uncle Pierce said.

"It is a city in layers," I said. I was trying to picture it from the outside and reconcile it with what we were seeing on the inside.

"Yes, and it goes down twelve layers beneath the surface of the mountain. "It spreads out beyond the base of the mountain, underground."

"The map shows fourteen levels," my dad said.

"Most of the underground layers are not on that map," Uncle Pierce explained. "You would need the comprehensive map in order to see all the layers, but you don't have a reason to have that map yet."

I was very curious about this mysterious underground, and I made a point to plan to explore some of those underground layers, or levels, whatever they were.

"I can tell you just about anything you want to know about Mountain Veil City while we eat," Uncle Pierce said. "Are you hungry?"

We answered in unison: "Yes!"

"Let's go," Uncle Pierce said, leading us toward a door on the other side of the room.

"Sir?" a man said. He was sitting and looking at a computer screen and he had a worried look on his face.

"What is it, Dawson?" Uncle Pierce said, stepping over behind him.

"We just got another one of those strange transmissions," Dawson said, fiddling with his computer controls.

"What does it say?" Uncle Pierce asked, leaning in to

look closer at the screen.

"It is the same as they have all been over the past week or so," Dawson said, "but I cannot figure it out. It is in code."

"The exact same message? Can anyone decode it?" Uncle Pierce said. "Did you ask Sumpter and Shushush?"

"I asked them, and they don't know. No one can break the code. We have put it through all the computer decoding programs and we just can't break it."

"Can you get any of it?" Uncle Pierce said.

"Not to make any sense of it," Dawson said, shaking his head.

"Maybe I can figure it out," I volunteered.

Uncle Pierce and Dawson laughed.

"This is a highly encrypted code," Uncle Pierce said. "Our top decoders have not been able to break it and they have been working on it for more than a week."

"Can I try?" I asked. "This is what I was doing back at the Complex."

Uncle Pierce and Dawson looked hesitantly at each other. I wondered how much they knew about the Complex.

"Come on, Pierce, let her try," my dad said. "Remember how she used to be so good at solving puzzles?"

"Just let me try?" I said, attempting to give Uncle Pierce my most intelligent look, yet aware that I must have looked ridiculous.

"What can it hurt?" my dad asked.

"Are you sure you don't want to go eat first?" Uncle Pierce said. "We can get a printout and you can take it back to your quarters to work on it."

I had a feeling he was teasing with me.

"Let me just take a look now," I said, "and then I can mull it over while we eat."

Uncle Pierce and Dawson laughed again, this time even harder than before.

"Is it okay?" Dawson asked Uncle Pierce.

"Sure, go ahead," Uncle Pierce said. "You can have five minutes then we will go eat and you can mull it over."

Uncle Pierce stepped away from the screen so I could sit on a stool beside Dawson. As soon as I saw the pattern of the scrambling, I knew what it said. This was very familiar to me. I read it out loud.

"A water closet on the cow's leg," I said.

"That is not what it says!" Dawson protested.

"That's what it says," I insisted, turning around to face Uncle Pierce and my dad. "I know that is what it says."

"That doesn't mean anything," Uncle Pierce said, shaking his head. He smiled at me. "You can't just make things up like that, Sweetheart."

"I am not making it up," I said forcefully. "The message is for me."

"What do you mean?" Uncle Pierce asked, suddenly serious.

"This message is for you?" my dad asked, stepping closer to the screen. "Does it have anything to do with the device you put on a cow's leg?"

"My friend, Kenrick, sent this message hoping I would receive it," I explained, nodding my head.

"But what does it mean?" Dawson said, looking into my face, as if to see if I were really telling the truth.

"He is trying to contact me," I said. "How can I send him a message?"

"You can just speak it and we can automatically scramble it," Dawson said.

"No, I want to make my own code," I said. "Can I type it, or should I speak the letters and symbols?"

"Just type it on this keyboard," Dawson instructed. "We won't scramble it when we send it out."

I was aware that everyone was watching every move I was making, every symbol I was typing. I carefully selected in order specific letters and symbols so that when Kenrick decoded the message he would know it was from me. I told him: "Moo, found dad, now living hidden city. No goat cheese."

"How do I send it?" I asked Dawson.

"What does it say?" Dawson asked.

"It is really just for Kenrick," I said, secretly glad that he was unable to decode it.

"We need to know what it says before we send it," Uncle Pierce said.

"I told him I am still alive," I said, omitting most of my message.

"Okay, press that button to send without scrambling," Dawson said.

I pushed the button.

"How long do we have to wait for a reply?" I asked.

"It could be hours or days before he gets it," Uncle Pierce said. "Then he could take weeks to respond. Come on, let's go eat."

I stood up and turned away from the computer, delighted that I was able to receive and decode a message that was just for me!

We began walking toward the door.

"Good job, Layla," my dad said, putting his arm around me.

"I have to admit, I am quite impressed," Uncle Pierce said. "I still am not sure about the meaning, but you were able to decode that thing in a matter of seconds. I may be able to get you a job upstairs too."

I beamed with satisfaction as we approached the door.

CHAPTER 14

"Sir!" Dawson called.

Uncle Pierce stopped, with his hand nearly touching the panel to open the door.

"What is it, Dawson?" he asked, turning back to face him.

"We just got another message!" Dawson yelled. "This one is different!"

I was back at the computer screen in two seconds flat.

"Let me see it!" I said, staring at the screen.

The scrambled message appeared and, although it was coded in three layers, I instantly was able to decode it. As soon as I read it, I felt faint.

"I found your mother."

a novel by Dana Pride

A global disaster, known as The Great Devastation, drastically changed life on earth. Layla, a Kidgen, or Kid-Genius, is living and working at the Complex, where the Insiders have everything they need provided for them: jobs, food, clothing, entertainment. Layla is aware of the Outsiders, (the Ordinaries, the Crims, the Chairs and the Runners) who are just scraping by without the use of technology, but she doesn't have any reason to think much about them - until Kenrick, one of her friends who is also a Kidgen and a Comgen (Computer-Genius), secretly arranges for four friends to travel.

Suddenly Layla becomes curious. What is life Outside really like? Where will they go? What will they eat? Will they be able to get back safely and unpunished? Kenrick has a few surprises in store for them, especially for Layla, whose life will never be the same after they make their journey Outside the Complex.

Novels by Dana Pride
- » *So How is THAT a Bully?*
- » *After the Great Devastation*
- » *The Red Cloak*
- » *Nightmares of Murder*
- » *No One Like You*
- » *Existing*
- » *All These Things*
- » *Kissing a Dead Man*

Non-fiction books by Dana Pride
- » *How to Get Fat Without Even Trying*
- » *What Really Happened in Mexico*

Poetry books by Joseph Fram
- » *Joseph's Journey, Volume 1*
- » *Joseph's Journey, Volume 2*
- » *Joseph's Journey, Volume 3*
- » *Joseph's Journey, Volume 4*
- » *Joseph's Journey, Volume 5*
- » *Joseph's Journey, Volume 6*
- » *Joseph's Journey, Volume 7*
- » *Joseph's Journey, Volume 8*

Other titles available:
- » *Moses' Chisel by Steven Martin*
- » *Nathan is Nathan, by Jahla*
- » *Nathan Art: Autistic-Artistic by Nathan*

Now also available to download as e-books!

http://everlastingpublishing.org

http://danabooks.8k.com

Everlasting Publishing
PO Box 1061
Yakima, Washington 98907
USA